MURD...
A LONG TI...

Anthony Masters

Constable · London

First published in Great Britain 1991
by Constable & Company Limited
3 The Lanchesters, 162 Fulham Palace Road
London W6 9ER
Copyright © 1991 Anthony Masters
The right of Anthony Masters to be
identified as the author of this Work
has been asserted by him in accordance
with the Copyright, Designs and Patents Act 1988
ISBN 0 09 470360 4
Set in Palatino 10pt by
CentraCet, Cambridge
Printed in Great Britain by
Redwood Press Limited
Melksham, Wiltshire

A CIP catalogue record for this work
is available from the British Library

To
MILES
in renewal
of an old
and trusted
friendship

Prologue

The cherry trees were in blossom on the morning they died. It was dawn and their delicate fragrance was in the misty air, along with the hint of lavender and herbs. They crossed the Provençal orchard quietly, their hands bound, their guards following. The interrogation had been short, the accusations damning – and their protests had been stilled by blows. They were hardly more than boys and their terrified parents and relatives were not allowed to accompany them to the place hurriedly chosen for their execution.

The mist was fleecy and translucent and the path through so familiar to all of them. They had played here as children; taken the girls of St Esprit here as adolescents. Now their footsteps were muffled on the flinty path for the last time. A light, darting breeze brought petals floating down and a few settled in the young men's hair. Most of them were smoking cigarettes given to them by their captors and they greedily drew the smoke deep inside them. No one spoke and the sigh of the dying wind stilled the slender branches of the cherry trees. Some of the young men had Roman names – Octavius, Sylvain, Antonius, Petronius. There were six of them, numbed, unbelieving, innocent of anything except lust and selfishness and natural curiosity. Still they could not understand, not accept. They were like the trees, stilled now, without alarm.

At the end of the orchard was a stile and beyond it a grassy field. There, a woman waited, shivering a little in the early morning stillness. The fragrance from the nearby lavender fields increased as their captors nudged them on. There was no commanding officer; it was to be a quick, revengeful business – an example to the community.

They were pushed towards a corner of the field and put into a single line. A German soldier took a photograph, then another. Still no one spoke. The wind came back and the mist rolled over the olive grove beyond, making the stunted trees insubstantial. A twisted limb appeared here and there – and then was gone.

'We haven't *done* anything.' His voice burst out, cracked and coarse in the stillness. 'We haven't done anything,' he repeated, more muted, more helplessly accepting.

'Please,' whimpered another. 'Please – '

Suddenly, the woman who had been watching ran forward and stood in front of the line of young Frenchmen.

'Kummel would never authorise this,' she shouted. 'You can't just mow them down – '

'How do you know what his orders are?' one of the Germans sneered. 'Or shouldn't we enquire?'

There was a burst of laughter and then a long pause. The woman still stood there uncertainly, but, ignoring her, the German soldiers assembled in a ragged line. There were eight of them – only a year or so older than their victims. The wind came for the third time, and with it the fusillade of shots. The noise seemed to go on for a very long time and the young men crumpled and fell. The last to go was the woman, who fell slowly, finally embracing the earth. The grass rustled, the wind leapt and died – leapt and died again. Then, the shots ceased.

Slowly, a German soldier put down his gun, took his camera out of his tunic pocket and began to photograph the bodies.

1

The house and gardens were still, somnolent in the afternoon heat. Marius walked slowly down the tiled path to the walled garden, dreading what he was going to find in the old conservatory. There had only been two scrawled notes so far. He had torn them both up, but another was bound to follow. Of course, he had seen him. Trespassing. That was why he didn't hurry as he had done the other times. He knew what the note would say. There was no point in seeing it sooner than he had to.

A bee circled in front of him, lazily inscribing a long loop in the drowsy, pollen-hazed air. Marius glanced behind him at the faint noise of the drawing-room doors opening and closing. It was the old woman. His mother. Come out to sniff the heady aroma of the sun-baked garden, like an old cat sensing comfort. Maybe memory even. Since the stroke she had lost her identity, her clarity, so much of her mind. But maybe the basking flowers and the dusty shrubs might stir some dim sensation in Solange's dulled consciousness. The house with its four cupolas, ivy-strangled walls, flaking grey shutters and overgrown, weed-choked flower-beds seemed a suitable wilderness background to her own husk of a being. She stumbled through the long grass on the drive, childishly looking about her. Marius quickened his pace. He didn't want her to amble after him.

In front of the Château Letoric was a small ornamental lake with a fountain at its centre. In its heyday, the cherub spouted water from a pouting mouth, but now its mouth was jammed with rotting vegetation and water creepers clung to its stone body like vines. The lake still had water in the centre, but the edges were thick with reeds and weed and bulrushes.

Now as Marius opened the conservatory door, he was struck by the virulent buzzing of copulating insects which filled the humid air inside. He smelt geraniums, mint, decay all in one compressed perfume. Deliberately procrastinating, he looked ahead. Beyond the conservatory was the overgrown garden. Beyond that the forest that stretched to Viles.

Sure enough the note was there, spiked by a garden fork. A typically melodramatic symbol, worthy of Jean-Pierre. The wine Marius had taken at lunchtime suddenly rose in his throat like bile and he began to shake somewhere inside – somewhere that hurt. At forty-eight Marius had thought he was immune to emotional shock, and certainly the reaction to Jean-Pierre's first two clumsily scrawled notes had been comparatively low-key. The hurt had not lingered. But when Marius began to realise how serious he was, he knew that everything in his world was at risk. Essentially Monique would not be able to accept what had started all those summers ago.

The note read: 'GIVE ME WHAT I'M OWED – OR EVERYONE WILL KNOW.' And what Jean-Pierre considered himself owed was 250,000 francs.

Marius scrumpled up the cheap notepaper. He would see Jean-Pierre and stop all this childishness right away. Quietly, severely, he would tell him that he was committing a criminal offence and that whilst he was prepared to overlook it, to put it down to the crude act of a crude mind, he was not going to allow it to happen again.

His curious, new-found confidence put Marius in a defiant mood. He shoved the paper into the pocket of his corduroy trousers and moved outside into the turgid sun again. It seemed, if anything, to be even hotter. A butterfly darted from behind a lavender bush and the sweet musky smell made him feel light-headed. The memories flooded his mind with erotic recollection. It had been here on the long soft grass that they had first made love so many years ago. He'd been a boy when it started. Both the same age. Both wanting the same thing. Not needing to ask, just drawn together by instinct. The garden was more or less the same as it had been then: overgrown, the grass slightly rank, moon daisies growing amidst the wilderness,

10

unpruned roses straggling up the walls. Marius began to shake again. But this time not out of fear. Despite himself some of the old desire had returned.

'I've never known what collaboration really means.'

'It all seems clear to me,' said André.

'Does it?'

Annette and André Valier were sitting in the back garden of their home in St Esprit. Theirs was a tall elegant house in a street of tall elegant houses. Shuttered, balconied, plastered – all were inhabited by the professional people who had decided to live in the small-town atmosphere of St Esprit, conveniently near Aix yet with a charm of its own.

André was editor of the *Journal Discours* with an office in Aix. He was dark-haired, slender, with rather a fidgety little goatee beard – an affectation that had always irritated her, just as his tendency to lecture her did. When she had first met him they had both been at the Sorbonne and André had been very much the successful student, clever with politics, clever with social manipulation, surrounding himself with his own élite group of sycophants and acolytes. He played the intellectual grasper and she, as a shy innocent from a devout Catholic family, had felt privileged to be allowed entry to André's circle – and later to his bed. But over the years he had become drier; more provincially than nationally ambitious; a big fish in a murky pool – while she had lost her faith and gathered small-town sophistication.

Annette ran a high-class local restaurant. Uneasily childless, they had filled their lives with friends and food, ideas and conversation, wine and discussion. They were still young, still in their thirties, with enough money to enjoy foreign travel. And then there was golf and the Press Club in Aix. The restaurant was quite a social focus too, so they had little time to themselves, and the frantic pace of their lives dowsed the pain of twelve years of failed conception. The failure had started out as a surface wound between them, but now it was deepening, beginning to fester.

Today, the recently revived Larche affair dominated their conversation. Most people in St Esprit had spent months talking

11

about it, and *Journal Discours* had not only run some contentious leading articles on the affair but had also had its correspondence columns filled with the suddenly released voices of those who had harboured fermenting bitterness and suspicion.

'It all comes down to the same thing in the end,' André continued. 'They've had nothing else to think about since the war.'

'It's 1990,' she said. 'Forty-five years. A long time.'

'Yes – it is a long time. But time here is different. Haven't you noticed?'

He sounded faintly mocking and she looked up sharply. The mocking note had only entered his voice recently, and it was combined with an impatience that Annette found increasingly threatening. Ever since she had been so summarily dismissed from Henri Larche's employ, André had been disappointed in some way she couldn't understand. As much as he tended to get on her nerves, she clearly was now beginning to dissatisfy him. Annette couldn't understand what she had done; after all the restaurant by the river was very successful, and what had been so special about working for a retired judge who was writing a dowdy family history? Far less interesting than running a restaurant, she thought defensively.

'We've been here ten years, André. I can hardly remember Paris.'

'Things happen in Paris. Nothing has *really* happened here since the war; nothing of any note, nothing to remember.'

'That's nonsense.'

'Is it? What did Giono write about Provence?' He got up and went into the house, leaving her with the depressing certainty that he was going to read to her – and then lecture. Maybe we should have more people around, she thought. Maybe they should limit the times they spent together although, God knows, they were limited enough already. They always seemed to be surrounded by people. She reached for her bag and took out a small mirror and stared critically into it. Drawn-back dark hair, large brown eyes, good complexion. Less favourable points then obtruded. There was a hint of sallowness, lines around the mouth, a droop to the chin. Was he going with someone else, she suddenly wondered. Was their mutual inability to conceive finally driving him away? All the little irritations and contemptuous impatience – was that what it meant? The first shock of the idea made her tremble in the swamping heat. She longed for the Mistral to blow, longed for something to shatter the calm. That was the problem with their lives. The calm. Like St Esprit. The town lived – had lived – too long in calm waters. Its inhabitants were thirsting for change. And perhaps – perhaps André was too.

She had never told André the real reason that Henri Larche had sacked her. But she knew it was because she had read Marie Leger's letter to him in all its filth and candour. He couldn't bear her knowing. She had been amazed herself. Amazed and frightened. But it was all over now and she admired her own enterprise with the restaurant even if André didn't, patronising her with his distant interest.

He was coming out now, book in hand, his face wreathed in the self-indulgent smile of the man with the captive audience. His beard almost wagged with complacency.

'Listen. "All civilised people see the day beginning at dawn or a little after or a long time after or whatever time their work begins; this they lengthen, according to their work, during what they call 'all day long' and end when they close their eyes. It is they who say the days are long. On the contrary, they are round."'

'Yes,' said Annette dutifully. 'In Provence the days *are* round. I've never felt their length – even in the restaurant.'

'The days are long in Aix,' he replied. 'They don't worry about collaborators there. There's too much to do.'

'Maybe in round days the past isn't so far away,' she ventured. 'Maybe the 1940s are as near as the 1990s.'

'I think that's true.' He was no longer mocking, back to his old self. But who was that other person inside him? The one who was growing tired of her?

'You never explained,' she said quietly.

'Explained what?'

'You said collaboration was all too clear to you.'

'Well, so it is to anyone,' he began patronisingly. 'During the German occupation most people colluded with the occupying forces in some small way or the other simply by living and eating and drinking and going about their daily business. But there were some who actually *aided* the German occupation.

13

They were the traitors. Some were caught right away; others confessed later. But some continued in public office unsuspected. If it hadn't been for the Lyon trial nothing would have happened. Larche would have retired safely. No accusations were made. A minor war criminal – an old Nazi – half crazy, demented, talked about a Frenchman heading up that tribunal. He never mentioned Larche's name, but the tongues have been wagging ever since.'

'I *know* Henri Larche. He is a man of honour. I can't help feeling that the *Journal* stirred it up again,' she said flatly.

'You mean *I* did.'

The tension between them was back. In all their years of marriage, Annette had never criticised André's editorial integrity. Now, in a few seconds, the conversation had become a weapon in her hands. Why? Was it his earlier mockery? Her own suspicions of the person inside him? And was she going to use the weapon? Annette wiped perspiration from her brow. 'You let it through,' she accused.

'Daudein's a good journalist.'

'He dug it up again.'

'He only wrote about what was there.'

'There was *nothing* there. Just rumours.' Annette paused. She could back off now. But again she continued. 'All your tame sleuth did was to dig up dirt – and there's plenty of it in this town.'

'When local rumour suggested Larche might have presided over an unofficial tribunal that executed half a dozen young men from this town. We had to investigate.'

'Larche denies everything.' She paused. 'Those young men murdered a German officer – it was the Germans who killed them.'

'It seems they may well have wanted a respectable civilian – a judge, say, to give the tribunal some hint of respectability.'

'Isn't it better to forget it all? Safer?'

'For who?'

'Everybody. It's too long ago – even if the days *are* round.'

'I don't think it is.'

'He's an old man.'

'There are many old people who remember.'

'And he has a wife who was a heroine in the Resistance.'

14

'There's an irony.'

'She was badly tortured.'

'Another irony.' André's voice was strained now, but so was hers.

'She's ill.'

'She doesn't know what's going on. This won't harm her.'

'It'll hurt his son,' she snapped.

'Marius? He's a policeman. Interpol. He should be able to understand everyone's concern.'

'I *know* them. Remember? They're people to me – vulnerable people.'

There was a long silence between them while they both thought of their real bone of contention. Annette knew they weren't really arguing about Henri. They were sparring, hoping to hurt, fighting round the deep pit of their childless lives and the desiccation of their personalities.

'I'm merely stating all the facts. I'm sure he'll accept that all the facts about his father should be revealed. After all, it could clear his name.' André was blandly reasonable.

'Facts? They're all rumours.'

'Facts will emerge.' He sounded almost pompous now.

'Half the letters are anonymous.'

'I never knew you cared so much.' He was genuinely surprised.

'I don't,' she said quietly and almost told him what she did care about. She stared up at André, wondering if he was about to do the same. The silence between them lengthened.

'You are not making progress. You should be asking more questions, trying to clear my name. The point is – as I never headed that tribunal, who did? Everyone should be regarded as a possible traitor; everyone who was in a public position at that time.' Henri spooned omelette into his mouth. It was runny, under-cooked, and in the dim, shadowed light of the high-ceilinged dining-room, the food looked palLid and inedible. At the other end of the table sat Solange. In the middle, Marius. Early dinner had become a habit, served by Estelle, the only family retainer left, who creaked out from St Esprit every day on her black-framed relic of a bicycle. His parents were recluses now: Solange because of her illness; Henri because of his shame. Marius found it curious that Estelle still grimly came to offer her half-cooked cuisine. The other servants – the housekeeper and the gardener – had long since departed, shortly after the Lyon trial. Excuses had been made: age, family responsibilities, fatigue, ailments – the list was endless. His father, originally incapable of cooking, made little messes and a nurse would call occasionally to see Solange.

'She's wandering in her mind, monsieur,' she had told Marius. 'But she'll be able to live at home for a little while longer. It's as well to keep the old people together as long as we can, isn't it?' He had nodded but inwardly disagreed. Away for long periods, each time he returned home, Marius felt sure he would find that one of them had dropped dead or that Letoric had burned down around them. He planned to sell the house as soon as he could get the permission from Henri which had so far been withheld. Marius wanted to install both of them in sheltered housing in St Esprit, but Henri refused on the grounds of the wagging tongues. He has a point, thought Marius grimly, as he often did.

'I'm seeing quite a few of them very soon,' he replied to his father's remark after a long silence. In fact he had already seen Mireille Leger – and been quite unable to penetrate her calm unyielding exterior. She had told him she didn't know anything – and had continued to repeat the phrase until the end of an unsatisfactory conversation.

'Not soon enough. I'm being slandered all over again – it's building up. That damned paper – '

'Is it Estelle who's been telling you?'

'Who else? I never go out.'

'She's got no right – ' he began.

'She's my only contact with the outside world.'

'There's always me, Father.'

'You tell me what you think will please me.'

Marius looked at the bottle of wine on the table. It seemed the only substantial thing in the room, what with the rickety old people and the equally rickety furniture. Family portraits hung dourly from the walls and a glass chandelier tinkled with muffled resonance. Dozens of photographs covered small marquetry tables that huddled against the walls and in the huge, tiled fireplace was a dusty arrangement of dried flowers. The air smelt of old polish and the herbs that used to hang in the kitchen and were now long gone. It was a perfume he would always associate with the Château Letoric – his beloved home that he was now being forced to sell before it finally dropped to pieces in front of his eyes, taking his helpless parents with it.

He looked at his father. There was a kind of vulnerable distinction to him. He had originally been tall, slim, with a long hawk-like face that had flashed smiles at him when he was a child – smiles that had only appeared for an instant, as if they were purely, privately for him. Then Marius looked across at his mother, her hunched, shapeless figure over-wrapped despite the heat and her leonine head lowered over her plate, her face wiped clean of any expression. She played with the omelette on her plate, occasionally mumbling to herself. They had both had a long old age, he thought, and now they were crumbling like the house around them.

What did he really feel, he wondered. For his mother – only a desire for her to die. She had been a remarkable woman, with her rich laughter and anecdotes, her fine intellect and the intelligence in her eyes. And, of course, her bravery; her spirit had been legendary, unbroken by the Gestapo and the searing physical pain they inflicted on her. She had never talked about the torture or her torturers and had always been careful not to expose to him as a child the marks on her body. But once she had left the bathroom door unlocked and Marius, for a brief accidental instant, had seen what they had done to her. Her breasts and stomach were a mass of small scar tissue and her shoulders bore longer, crueller stripes. It was only when he was older that Marius realised that not only had the Gestapo whipped her, but they had stubbed out their cigarette ends on her as well.

As for his father, he didn't know what to think. Like his mother, Marius had loved him to distraction, but he had always been that little bit more remote. For so many years his father had been a local dignitary, an associate of the mayor, a presider over committees, a giver of distinguished dinner parties, a man of importance. How would he preside over a kangaroo court? And yet a German officer had been murdered. How did this square with the law, despite the occupation? These questions

17

had circled in his mind ever since the Lyon trial and he had come to no resolution for the simple reason that he had known only one tiny part of his father – the minute area reserved for him – and so therefore had hardly known him at all. And as for the querulous old man that he had now become? His hopeless misery, his reclusive existence, his protestations, his vulnerability had worn a hole in Marius's heart and it hurt. It also enraged him. He loved St Esprit – and he hated St Esprit. More so now that its febrile clutches, its festering memory was reaching out to his father. And was he, Marius, dragging his feet? Certainly he wanted to clear his father's name. But what if he began asking questions professionally – the way he had been trained to ask questions. That was something Marius was afraid to do, for fear of what he might find out. For Marius had no real idea whether his father was guilty or not.

He spooned more omelette in. It's practically raw, he thought. We'll all die of salmonella poisoning. He poured more of the heavy velvet claret into his glass, knowing he was beginning to drink too much but justifying it, putting it down to stress, to the action that he was prevaricating over.

'Do you never answer a question?' asked his father sourly.

'I didn't realise it *was* a question,' Marius defended himself. 'I've never tried to minimise the effect of what is being said, but most of what *is* being said is very trivial. And ill-informed.'

'I never presided over such a court.' He thumped the scarred table with a veined fist. 'I never *would* preside over such a court. You must ask more questions. Follow up every lead. Stop that damnable newspaper. Don't you understand? It's all flaring up again. I can't take any more of it.'

'Now Matthieu – stop losing your temper.' The old woman's voice was furred and slow and ineffably weary.

'I am *not* Matthieu,' he exclaimed. 'That was your brother.'

'Eat up your food,' she said dreamily. 'It's your favourite – that blancmange.'

'It happens to be an omelette.'

'Don't gulp it down.'

'I was actually picking at it.'

'I'll give you a dollop of raspberry jam.'

'In God's name – '

Marius smiled ruefully. They often had these mad conversations now. She was locked into a distant, splintered past; he in the frustrated anger of the present.

'And what are you laughing at, Marius?'

'I was smiling.'

'At two old fools?'

'No – at a misunderstanding.'

'That's all my life,' he pronounced, pushing away the omelette, reaching for the wine. Marius looked at the brown age spots all over his hands. They clustered there like kisses from death. Marius shook his head, trying to clear away the wine-ridden thoughts. He was becoming maudlin.

'What *are* you doing on my behalf?' the old man asked. He was no longer aggressive, simply pathetic now with the whine in his voice.

'I'm going to see Valier as well. He's the man who's been stirring up the trouble with this damned gutter journalism. I've made an appointment with the new mayor in St Esprit – and I've spoken to Rodiet on the phone.'

'Gabriel Rodiet? He blames me for the execution of his mother. What is the point of talking to him?'

'Because he is Chief of Police. He knows the town.'

'And does he believe you? Believe my innocence?'

'He's got an open mind.'

'That's not enough.'

'It'll have to do for the time being. And I saw one of the Leger sisters. They're not exactly our best friends.'

'What did you see them for? You keep talking to our enemies. It was one of those old bitches who sent me those filthy letters after the Kummel trial, making the accusation. Kummel *never* mentioned my name.'

'I know, Father,' said Marius wearily. 'Surely you realise that. We've been through it a thousand times.'

'You can't be sure of *anything* round here.' The old man took a pull at his claret.

Only once had they spoken about the other horrendous accusation in Marie Leger's first letter. 'You would never have done those unspeakable things with that filthy peasant Claude,' his father had stated rather than asked.

'Of course not, Father,' Marius glibly lied.

19

'I'm sorry to have asked you, Marius,' he had said, deeply ashamed.

Now, his father spoke hurriedly. 'You'll be talking to Annette next.'

'No, I shall avoid that. But you did her an injustice.'

'She didn't suit me any more.'

'You could have given her notice. Not sacked her on the spot.'

'I told you. She didn't suit. What more do I have to say? And there's no point in raking up the past.'

'That's what they're all doing.'

'Yes.' He nodded. 'Who knows who I can trust? *You* probably don't believe me. You're like Rodiet. You've got an open mind.'

'No. You're my father. If you say you didn't do it – and you've always denied it – then you didn't do it,' said Marius, conscious that he had denied his encounter with Jean-Pierre with the same authority as his father had denied heading the tribunal.

'Anyway, you'll be off soon. Back to that smart flat of yours in Lyon. While we rot here.'

'I've got another fortnight. This, believe it or not, is my summer vacation. And as for rotting, if we sold up you could have excellent – '

'Sheltered accommodation in that tower of babel? Are you mad?'

'Or elsewhere.'

'I'm not being run out of this town.'

Marius closed his eyes. I will not have another glass, he thought. As he poured it out, he smiled across the table at his father and for a few seconds his crumpled features were replaced by that old hawk-like face, rapacious in its intensity. Well, at least the wine blunted reality – and brought back memories more sharply. For a while. But how long could he defy his own integrity by being so professionally inert?

His mother belched and Estelle banged her way in.

'Fruit tart,' she announced, producing a glazed plastic confection straight from St Esprit's supermarket.

The two old people nodded as if before a schoolboy feast. But Marius could only call for the cheese.

*

'Mireille.'

'What do you want now?' Mireille's voice was sharp.

'I was looking for my writing case.'

'I haven't seen it.'

'I just wondered.'

Marie ambled through the small sitting-room of the lodge on the edge of the Ste Michelle estate, a dumpy little woman in a blue overall. She looks like a peasant, thought Mireille, a real peasant. Then she reminded herself that her twin sister might just as well look that way, for they had been reduced to being peasants anyway. Practically.

They were not identical twins. Marie had always been dumpy but Mireille was spare, brown as a nut, trim in her early sixties. Together they ran a dried flower business, creating posies and baskets of every size and colour. They grew and dried the flowers themselves, and also the herbs for the aromatic cushions they made as a sideline. The Leger sisters' sole means of transport was an ancient, battered Deux Chevaux which was the bane of the local garage.

Regretting her impatience Mireille asked her sister to sit down. There was a kinder note in her voice and, surprised, Marie did as she was told, spreading herself in the shabby old leather armchair. The room was over-furnished with heavy tables and a good deal of unfortunate wicker-work. The lights were dim and the wallpaper, an undistinguished mêlée of roses, clashed with the myriad of pictures – some oval, some oblong, all showing one aspect or another of a large château whose gravelled drive swept down to a forest track.

'It's getting late, dear,' said Marie.

Mireille looked at her watch. It was just after ten. 'I want to talk. Will you have a liqueur?'

'Not with my digestion.'

'Then I will. I shall have a Framboise.'

'Are you sure, dear? After all, you know you never sleep after – '

'I shall have a Framboise.'

'Very well.' Marie set her face against the problems drink caused her sister.

When she had resumed her seat Mireille said, 'I saw Larche yesterday afternoon.'

'Why didn't you tell me?' She was instantly both agitated and indignant. Mireille sighed. She was going to be her usual difficult self. Unlike most twins, Mireille felt light years apart from her sister, but it was more wish than actuality, for she could read Marie very well and she knew Marie could read her.

'Because I wanted to think.'

'We could have shared – '

'Now we are.'

'So you saw Henri – '

'No, you fool. I saw Marius.'

'There's no need to snap.'

'I'm sorry.' Mireille sought for strength. She had to control herself; she didn't want the predictable argument that would send Marie snivelling to bed.

'What did he want?'

'To justify his father.'

'To *defend* his father?'

'No, he wanted to know if we had proof – if anyone had proof.'

'And if not – to shut up?'

'No. He was probing. But reasonable.'

'You think – he believes in his father's guilt?' Her voice was excited. She always got worked up over crime, thought Mireille. Even petty crime. And since the Larche scandal had been raked up again, she was in her element. Mireille hated her sister for her provincial muck-raking; she loved her for her bumbling helplessness. It was an awkward combination of emotions and one that gave her much pain.

'No. He believes in his father's innocence – because his father has told him that he is innocent.' Mireille's voice was very controlled.

'He's guilty,' replied Marie with relish.

'That's your opinion.'

'And the opinion of everyone else in St Esprit.'

'A slight exaggeration – and there's no evidence whatsoever. Just talk. Ever since we lost Ste Michelle, you seemed to have this obsession that Larche was involved in some kind of conspiracy with Alain.'

'That bloody brother of ours – he's as big a crook as Henri.'

22

'A ludicrous statement,' said Mireille, sipping her Framboise.
'Henri is Alain's lawyer, and they've always been like brothers – much closer than Alain ever was to us. It stands to reason that Larche helped him.'

'Another sweeping statement – and we've had this conversation *so* many times. Don't you ever get tired of it?'

'You were as angry as I was; you're as embittered as I am.'

'Oh yes. I'm embittered all right. We lost the case and our share of the house and the land. And we're living in this slum and I have to listen to you going on and on about it.'

'It was all Henri's fault,' said Marie vehemently.

Mireille took another sip, feeling pleasantly detached, watching her sister's passion from a distance. 'Don't glare at me, Marie – it makes you look old.'

'I *am* old.'

'May I also remind you that you have reason to be *grateful* to Henri Larche?'

'Grateful?'

'He could have taken action – legal action – over those letters – those disgusting letters you wrote him.'

'I thought he should know his son was a poof – that he went with Jean-Pierre.'

'It was unforgivable.'

'Who are you to be so high and mighty?'

'I know what is right – and wrong – to do. You were wrong.'

There was a long silence between the two sisters. Marie scowled childishly. Mireille went on sipping her liqueur.

'What else did he ask?' Marie asked eventually. This time she spoke more reasonably. It was always the same, thought Mireille – the argument would subside into almost amicable bickering. It was as if the shouting was therapy for her.

'Oh, he was only trying to see what evidence – what hard facts – any local people had.'

'And you told him there was plenty?'

'I told him there were no hard facts. Only opinions – and rumours – and suspicions – in a small town where nothing has happened for years but a bloody war.'

'Enough for the *Journal* in Aix to take it up,' Marie pointed out.

The *Journal* had carried the headline on its middle pages –
WHO PRESIDED? And underneath, the tabloid clatter began:

> *Three years ago, Nazi war criminal Wolfgang Kummel told a
> court in Lyon that a high-ranking Frenchman had presided over a
> tribunal that . . .*

The machine-gun prose of the article stuttered on, naming no
names, intimating the Frenchman's rank was judge, calling on
local citizens to come forward and identify. That to do so would
be their duty. The final exhortation read:

> *The journal believes the collaborator is still amongst us. It is the
> duty of every citizen to bring him to justice.*

'That muck-raker Valier.' For the first time, Mireille looked
angry. 'He and that wife of his – they're both outsiders.'
'Now who's being narrow minded?' Marie looked at her in
delight now that she had found a weakness.
'What do you mean?'
'We've lived here all our lives. So have the Larches, come to
that. Anyone you distrust *has* to be an outsider.'
'Rubbish.'
'Why did you tell me all this anyway? You knew it would stir
me up,' Marie said abruptly.
'I don't like secrets – secrets corrupt.'
'Are you pleased you told me?'
'It was a duty.'
'You're so sanctimonious,' Marie sneered. 'What are you
doing?' she added sharply.
'Having another bloody Framboise.'
'I really must warn you – '
'And I'm taking it up to bed with me. Goodnight.'
Marie watched her sister leave the room in silence. She felt
suddenly exhausted, but beneath the exhaustion she was afraid.
How much did Mireille know? Could she have seen them
together?

*

The two old people were talking over cognac in their little sitting-room. It was a nightly ritual which they still maintained, despite Solange's meanderings and misunderstandings of time, place and people. Estelle would be forced to hover until Solange allowed herself to be helped up to bed. Just behind the room there was the kitchen with an ill-fitting serving hatch in between, and it was here that Estelle set up her listening post. Gradually over the months she had grown fascinated by the incongruity of the old people's conversation, mainly at cross-purposes but illuminated by sudden bursts of clarity. Most of the time Solange mumbled nonsense to which Henri would never respond. Instead he lay slumped in his chair, like an old lizard, she thought, his hooded eyes staring into the empty fireplace. Is he seeing ghosts, she wondered. Young men before a firing squad? Or wasn't he there after all?

Estelle would relay much of their conversations, such as they were, to Mariola Claude and they spent hours speculating over Henri's guilt. Their marathon gossip sessions, usually held in Mariola's aromatic kitchen, had chewed the subject to bits, but still they talked, happy in their assumptions, titillated by Estelle's access to Henri. Estelle lived alone, deserted by a mother she now never saw, and Mariola had stepped naturally into the emptiness. She saw Estelle as the daughter she had never had.

This evening, as Estelle made the coffee they would hardly drink, she listened to Solange's ramblings with half an ear, not surprised that Marius had settled for an early night.

'I'll go to St Denis tomorrow and see Jacques and Madeleine.'

'They're dead.' Henri's voice was flat and far away.

'I want to see that herb garden of theirs.'

'The house is sold.'

'She said she'd give me a recipe.'

'She's dead.'

'And I want to see if Jacques knows where Didier is.'

'You *know* where Didier is. He's safe. Out of harm's way.'

Estelle moved nearer the hatch. She had a sixth sense for Solange's more aware periods – and now she could feel one coming.

'I'd like to see Didier.'

'Soon.'

'It'll come out in the end, Henri.' Her voice was suddenly calm and sure.

'What will?' he asked impatiently.

'Didier knows it wasn't you.'

'Didier is very confused.'

'He could testify.'

Henri laughed, almost cackled. 'A madman?'

'Didier's with his mother.'

'He tried to kill her.'

'It was the Maquis that drove him. Every day, every hour – the constant fear.'

Her bursts of clarity were so sudden that they were alarming and Henri looked up at her curiously. 'You're right, of course.'

Behind the hatch Estelle moistened her lips. She would have something to tell her surrogate mother tomorrow.

2

Marius slept fitfully, one erotic dream following another in quick succession. The location was always the same. It was harvest time and he was out working with Jean-Pierre. The sun burnt down on the golden fields with a fierce and consistent heat that heightened at midday until it was almost unbearable. At midday they would stop the tractors and eat the simple meal that Madame Claude, Jean-Pierre's mother, had prepared for them. Salami. Bread. Wine. Fruit.

This was always how the dreams began, throbbing in the dusty searing heat of the fields. He saw Jean-Pierre, stripped to the waist, the sweat like oil on his body, the laughter in his eyes, his tongue licking the wine off his lips. Jean-Pierre lay back in the corn, his legs splayed out, his hands behind his head. And Marius was dragging himself towards him, his arms reaching out for him. Except that he was making no progress at all because a dead weight seemed to be pressing down on his legs, and the more he pulled towards Jean-Pierre, the heavier the weight seemed to be.

Sometimes he woke sweating. Then a light sleep would plunge him back into the struggle again. Towards dawn, he awoke again and put on the light. He got out a sheet of paper and began to write to Monique.

> My dearest,
> Here I am still making enquiries – even on holiday. The usual problem – made worse by the newspaper in Aix – my father's integrity. They are both much older in their different ways than when you met them in the winter. My mother is far gone, meandering about in her own world, quite impervious to anything

outside. She is no longer in touch with reality and has no knowledge of our impending marriage, or of anything else come to that. Father is beside himself with a curious mixture of rage and fear. Meanwhile the gossip about him is getting worse and I can't substantiate anything. I've never been able to get close to him, and it's difficult to do so now. It was bad enough after the Kummel trial, but this revival of interest is killing him. But the added complication is that I'm only playing at clearing his name – and I think he knows it. I suppose I don't want to find out the truth in case he is guilty. But I don't know how long I can go on with this farce, particularly as I feel his suffering so deeply.

It was good of you to offer to come down but I would prefer you not to; the house is a gloomy place and I am counting the days until I can be back with you in Lyon. There is an atmosphere here of such tension that you would be utterly miserable.

I used to love this house and would have wished to preserve it always. But now it's rotting around me all I want to do is to clean up, clear out and sell it to the first available buyer, having settled the elderly parents in some kind of sheltered housing. But will they move? They won't even think about it.

Anyway I've got a fortnight – a deadline I intend to keep. And during this time I really must try to resolve the situation about my father. Somehow I feel very unprofessional – an amateur sleuth rather than a member of Interpol. I just don't know how to handle it; although I have a local police contact, there is no path I could take that would be 'official'. So here I am, playing the ageing boy detective. It's so strange here – I'm finding I'm in the middle of a sort of role reversal. I was always close to Mother, but now she's as far away from me as she could be. And I hardly knew my father – yet now he's pathetically dependent on me waving some kind of magic wand and making it 'all right' again. We shall talk on the telephone soon.

All my love,

Marius

When he had finished, he closed his eyes and tried to sleep. But the painful scenes in the cornfield returned, sharper than ever before. Marius rose, took a whisky bottle out of the cupboard and poured an enormous draught into a tumbler. He drank it in two long spluttering gulps and then lay back. At last dreamless sleep enveloped him.

'What do you want with me at this time of night?'

'Come with me. We can't talk here.'

'Who let you in?' The old man sat on the edge of his bed, his shrunken figure in over-sized pyjamas. The bedroom, like every other room in the Château Letoric, had a very high ceiling. There were more pictures on the walls – mainly landscapes of the most traditional nature – and the wardrobes and chests of drawers were built on a massive scale, making the room claustrophobic despite its size. His unexpected visitor stood beside the bed.

'Your son.'

'He is awake?'

'I threw stones at his window – in the manner of the movies.'

'And where is he now?'

'He went back to bed.'

'Does he know why you're here?'

'Oh yes. He is very pleased that the matter is to be cleared up at last.'

'Well, he can't have been that pleased or he'd have come along with you,' the old man grumbled. 'And now you're asking me to get up and leave the house at this time of night. I'm too old for such capers.

'It's very important.'

'Why?'

'Everything's out now. You'll be exonerated.'

He looked incredulous, staring down at his watch. 'It's barely dawn.'

'I'm sorry about the early hour. I'm sure you'll agree it couldn't wait.'

'And I'm to be exonerated?' The old man looked up, a suspicious child.

'Yes, that's a promise.'

Henri gave a sudden chuckle and his mood changed. 'Lead on,' he said. 'I've been waiting a long time for this.'

*

'Where are we going?' Henri peered around him, hobbling a little. The house and overgrown grounds were grey in the shadowy dawn. A single bird sang from the walled garden.

'Not far – the conservatory.'

'Why did you make me creep out of my own house?' asked Henri indignantly, tripping over the uneven ground and almost falling. His visitor steadied him gently.

'We've got to keep it quiet for the moment – you'll see.'

'What am I to see? To hear?' A light breeze blew in their faces, soft, gentle, faintly scented. Above them a pale moon still hung in a lightening sky of scudding cloud.

'All in good time. Here we are.'

The breezes blew again, this time a little stronger. Henri shivered. 'I'm cold.'

'You'll think it's worth being cold when you hear what I've been able to do.'

Henri shuffled after his visitor into the cobwebs and overgrown vegetation of the conservatory.

'Well, tell me then,' he said rather querulously. 'I'm tired.'

His visitor sighed. 'I'm afraid we haven't got any more time,' he said.

'It's another glorious morning.'

'Isn't there a wind?'

'A bit of a one.'

'Not the Mistral?'

'*Not* the Mistral.'

'Ah well, I can face anything as long as it's not that. It makes me so bad-tempered.'

Isobelle Rodiet stretched and turned over in bed. She was a large, beautiful, languorous woman in her early sixties. At the dressing table her husband, Gabriel Rodiet, was straightening his tie. His well-cut light summer suit fitted his barrel-shaped body like a glove. Gabriel was a very well-fleshed man; not exactly fat, certainly not thin. His face was broad, blue-jowled after even the most recent shave, and his compact thatch of black hair was luxuriantly thick.

'I must go.'

'No breakfast?'

'I'll get some at the office.'

'Why so busy?'

'Just a lot on.' He came round and kissed her.

'Mm. What are you wearing?'

'My second summer suit, a shirt from La Florette, the tie I believe your mother gave me . . .'

'Idiot! I meant your aftershave.'

'The filth our daughter gave me.'

'She meant it for the best.'

'She bought it in a flea market.'

'Why wear it?'

'She'd find me out.'

'By the way, I meant to ask you. What did Marius Larche want yesterday?'

'What do you think?'

'His father's name, I suppose. Oh God – and he's such a nice boy.'

'Boy? The man's in his forties.'

'Yes, but he's boyish all the same. Fancy having to be a son to that horrible old man. I s'pose he thinks he didn't do it?'

'He has to,' said Gabriel shortly.

'You told him he did?' she asked.

'I told him I had no evidence to support an accusation.'

'Have you never thought of finding some? I would think it should be easy to get.'

'I doubt it. The town is full of rumour, that's all – like it always is.' The bedroom was bathed in sunlight, picking out the amber quilt, the pale sheen of the walnut dressing table, the pastel walls – all the beautiful shades and objects Isobelle had collected over the years of Gabriel's rising seniority.

'But you believe he did it?' she asked insistently.

'I keep an open mind.'

'Why? He as good as killed your mother.'

'She tried to intervene. That's all.'

'She tried to save those boys and the Germans shot her as a result of her intervention.'

'Don't let's have this conversation again, Isobelle,' he said wearily. 'It's bad enough with that wretched journalist stirring – '

'Don't you *care*?'

31

'You do all the caring for me. It's you who believes Henri guilty. Not me.'

'Gabriel . . .'

'Well?' said Gabriel bleakly.

'Why don't you want to nail the bastard?'

'I've known him a long time.'

'Is *that* the reason?'

'I've told you so many times before.' His voice was dull, emotionless. 'I have no evidence.'

She turned over again. 'You're not a man of hot blood.'

'Depends on the circumstances,' he said, kissing her cheek. 'See you tonight.'

'Get up!'

Jean-Pierre looked blearily at his mother.

'Get out of bed. You were drunk last night.'

'I'm drunk every night.'

'You'll lose your job.'

'Who cares?'

She bent over him, her dark, rather bewhiskered face only a few centimetres above his. He could smell the garlic on her breath. 'I care. We'll have no money. Look at you – your face is swollen. You haven't shaved. You used to be good-looking. Now you're drink-sodden.'

'Compliments won't get you anywhere, Maman.'

'He won't pay, you know.'

'He will. In time.'

'You know it's a criminal offence – what you're doing?'

'What are you on about now, Maman?' said Jean-Pierre impatiently.

'Haven't you forgotten he's a policeman? A high-up policeman.'

'All to the good. He won't want to admit what happened.'

'It was only a few times. Nothing. Not in this day and age. And what about you? What do *you* get up to when you go to Lyon? Leaving me here – '

'Don't start, Maman.' Jean-Pierre turned his face to the wall, closing his eyes against his mother's tirade. But he couldn't close his ears and he could still smell her breath.

'Don't spoil yourself,' she berated him. 'What would the Curé say?'

'He probably fancies boys himself.'

'You'll be struck down,' she said furiously. 'How can you blaspheme like this?' Then she continued more hesitantly, 'It was an adolescent business with Larche. It happens.'

'Adolescent? He's had me again and again.'

'Don't exaggerate.'

'I tell you I've helped him out – and not long ago,' he insisted.

'He *won't* pay, I tell you. At best it'll be in dribs and drabs.'

'He'll pay up eventually. It'll get us out of this hovel.' He looked round at the simple furniture of his bedroom.

'Hovel? This is our home – has always been our home.'

'And we could do better.'

'How can I help it? Your father left us nothing.'

'Yes, Maman,' said Jean-Pierre wearily.

She was silent now, staring down at him. 'If you're set on this business,' she said at last, 'you want to put the screws on him.'

Jean-Pierre rolled over, his mouth dry and his head pounding. 'I'm going to have a future,' he muttered. 'It's not always going to be like this.'

'Then put the pressure on,' she insisted.

Jean-Pierre looked up at her with a sudden perception he had not experienced in years. Behind the façade of his mother's persistent nagging, her impatient contempt for him, was someone else: a strong woman, far stronger than himself. Of course he knew this – had always known it – but he didn't think about her very often.

'You're right,' he said with a new respect. 'I'll not let Larche off the hook though. He used me.'

'Well, if you're going to do it,' she replied brusquely, 'squeeze him harder.'

She continued to urge him and Jean-Pierre closed his eyes as the words rattled over him like a shower of hail stones. Farm labourer and aged peasant mother, he thought miserably. Shackled to each other for all time. Or were they more like prisoner and jailer? But what would happen if Marius did pay up? Would that alter their relationship? Somehow Jean-Pierre had his doubts.

There was a knock at the door.

'Who's that?' he groaned, turning over again.

'Estelle.'

'That slut.'

'She's my friend.'

'You mean your chief source of scandal.' He grinned up at her but she wouldn't smile back.

'You don't understand women's talk,' she admonished and turned away from him, hurrying to answer the door.

As Jean-Pierre dozed and dreamily calculated, his mother and Estelle sat hunched over coffee cups in the old-fashioned kitchen. Nothing seemed to have been replaced in years; Mariola did most of her good country cooking on the open range and, despite their poverty, produced classic and magnificent dishes. Her only concession to modernity was an old-fashioned and violently humming fridge, which was wedged against the dark wall a little to the left of a huge and ornate dresser which housed Mariola's mother's china. A scrubbed kitchen table and battered store cupboards filled the remainder of the room. In the air hung the scent of past culinary successes and the good coffee they were now drinking. Estelle had finished relating the conversation she had listened to so intently between Henri and Solange and Mariola commented reflectively, 'Didier can't be trusted.'

'Who is he?'

'He's a tragedy,' said Mariola obscurely. 'Now he's locked up in an asylum near Aix. He nearly killed his mother.'

'Does anyone ever visit him?'

Mariola paused. 'I've been. Once I took Jean-Pierre. But Didier lives in his own world.'

'Is he violent?' asked Estelle with excited curiosity.

'They keep him sedated.'

'Does he know anything about Henri?'

'Perhaps he did once. He's very confused now.'

'But why? What drove him crazy?'

Mariola paused, savouring the moment. 'He was a brave young man – very young – only in his late teens when he

34

worked with Solange in the Maquis. Almost the same age as Commissaire Rodiet.'

Estelle leant forward, a child, wondering at the power of the storyteller, engrossed in a heady narrative.

'He had some terrible experiences. Before she went barmy, Solange told me he had been tortured by the Gestapo – just as she was. After the occupation ended he fell to pieces.' Mariola drank more coffee. 'Now he's like a shell.'

Estelle idly thought of an empty sea shell – the kind she might pick up on the beach. In her mind's eye she put her ear to it, wondering if she would hear the sound of the ocean. Instead she heard unmistakable cries of pain.

'Wake up.'

'Mm?'

'Wake up. The Boche have got him.'

Marius opened his eyes to find his mother standing over him. Her large breasts flopped out of her dressing gown.

'Oh God!'

'He's gone.' She was very agitated.

'Calm down. Cover yourself up.' Her lack of dignity was unbearable. She had always been so composed, regal even. Now her reserve had disappeared completely and he could see the scars.

'He's gone.' She tugged at his pyjama sleeve. 'Henri. They've taken him. Come and see.'

'What's the time?'

'Time?'

He searched on the floor and found his wrist-watch. 'It's after nine. He's gone for a walk.'

'I've been looking for him.' Her voice took on a more normal tone and Marius looked up sharply.

'Mother – if you're really worried – '

'Yes, I'm worried.'

'OK. Let me get dressed.'

She still stood in his bedroom, looking down at him.

'Let me get *dressed*.'

She sighed as she began to walk away.

*

35

Marius searched the house and then the grounds while she stood by the door, looking out helplessly. He left the conservatory until last because it had such bad associations for him. But finally he went there. It was just after ten and the Mistral had begun to blow. The heat was still intense, but the wind battered him relentlessly and the long unkempt grass rustled like a prairie.

His father lay on the floor of the conservatory. Never had Marius seen so much blood.

To see his father dead was so unbelievable that Marius simply stood and stared, unaware of time passing, looking fixedly into his father's dead eyes. They returned his gaze rigidly. He was lying on his back, a kitchen knife in his hands. Marius recognised it by the unusual design on the bone handle. It had an elephant carved into it. His father had sliced ham with it. Now he had slit his throat. The long thin line out of which so much blood had flowed was so neatly sliced that it was almost impossible to see the cut until he looked hard. The blood had flowed from the incision all over his dressing gown and down his pyjama trousers. There was so much that he looked almost festive. One hand clutched the knife; the other lay neatly at his side. I won't disturb anything, he thought. He's not just my father. He's my corpse.

Mother? Damn. He'd forgotten all about her. He should have known she would have wandered down here eventually. She was standing in the doorway, quite calm now, looking at her husband dispassionately.

'They've done it.'

'No – '

'Boche. Bloody Boche.'

'Mother. He's taken his own life.'

'They cut his throat. The pigs. In reprisal for me. We'll have to hide. Hide all the servants. They've been torturing me. I wouldn't say anything. Now they've done this.'

He took her arm and tried to lead her away, but she resisted. 'Come away. Now.' He was strict, authoritative. Despite this, she still didn't budge. 'Do I have to carry you?' he insisted.

Then she began to cry. No tears but just great hard dry sobs. 'Henri – I want you back. I want you back.' Her voice was muffled.

Eventually he managed to lead her away. On the way back to the house he met the slatternly Estelle, showing her thighs, mounted on a bicycle with a basket of doubtful-looking vegetables in front of her. She suddenly made him feel physically sick.

'What's happened?' she asked.

'My father. An accident.'

'Henri – he's dead.' Solange went up to Estelle like a child and laid her hands on her bicycle handlebars. 'They've murdered Henri.'

'Murdered?' Estelle repeated the words with deep, gloomy relish.

Too late, Marius remembered how much she loved death, funerals, illness – it gave her life meaning. He had privately nicknamed her the Chief Ghoul. Now she was in her element. Marius observed her closely, trying to keep the waves of shock at bay. But the horrendous image of his father's blood was sharp and distinct and could not be erased.

'Take her arm – '

'Murdered,' muttered Solange.

'Take care of her.'

'Me?' Estelle dismounted, showing more grey flesh, and leant her bicycle against the crumbling brickwork of the terrace which fronted the overgrown lake. It was very hot in the morning sun and he could smell her sweat.

'Yes. Take her into the house. Make her coffee. Give her brandy.'

'What are you going to do?'

'Phone the police.'

'But *you're* a policeman,' said Estelle stupidly.

'He's my father – I can't investigate this.' He still felt sick and a trembling was beginning behind his knees.

'Please!' The old woman was standing there like a patient old horse.

'Very well. Come on, dearie.'

'They killed him.'

'Come on, love. Let's have a brandy.'

Marius knew Estelle had automatically assumed that the offer of brandy definitely included her.

*

37

'Rodiet.'

Marius stood by the telephone in the hallway of Letoric. Bright sunshine flooded the grubby mosaic in great golden beams. Dust swirled in one of them and he stared at the translucent specks without speaking for a few seconds.

'It's Marius.'

'How are you?' His voice was a little vague.

'My father's dead.'

There was a short silence. Then: 'How?' Rodiet's voice was crisp.

'His throat's been cut.'

'I see.' He sounded impatient and Marius felt a stab of anger. Doesn't he understand what I'm saying – doesn't he know it's my father who's dead? My own father. Tears filled Marius'eyes for the first time since he had seen the slim pencil line cut in the withered throat.

'My mother. She came in. I didn't have much time to . . . Will you send someone?' His voice broke.

'I'll come myself. I'm very sorry.' Too late he was being conciliatory. 'When did you – '

'Just now. He's in the old conservatory.'

'I'll be a few minutes, and, Marius . . .'

'Yes?'

'Sit down. Don't go back in there.'

'I haven't touched anything.'

'Of course you haven't.'

'Forensic are on their way,' said Gabriel Rodiet gently.

They stood staring down at the old man. He looked like a bloodied doll. It was curious – he hardly resembled his father at all.

'Who will be in charge of the case?' asked Marius humbly.

'Lebatre. You know him?'

'No.'

'He's good.' Rodiet paused. 'I wouldn't say he's been dead very long. Doctor will tell us.'

A bee lazily buzzed over Henri Larche's dead white nose.

'The old lady?' asked Gabriel. 'What about her?'

'The domestic's helping to take care of her.'

'How's she taken it?'

'Confused. She knows he's dead.'

'And you?'

'I don't believe it.'

'Do you want to leave it all to me?'

'No. I want to get used to it.'

Marius had never liked Gabriel. Not because he had disliked his father, not because he had been such a very young Resistance hero and had known his mother in her heyday – but because he had never come out on either side. He was too fair, too anxious to be even-handed. In addition, his bullish approach grated on Marius, as did his sympathy. Even now he was putting a hand – a hairy paw – on his own. God damn him.

'Wouldn't you be better inside?'

'No.'

'Very well.'

There was a short contemplative silence. Then Gabriel said, 'What are your thoughts on this?'

'I'm not on duty. This is my father,' Marius spat out at him.

'I'm sorry.' Gabriel was penitent, which infuriated him even more. 'Of course it's all so . . . They'll be here soon.'

3

They came in a burst of wailing sirens and melodramatically screaming tyres on what was left of the gravelled drive. What a performance, thought Marius – and performance it certainly was. Even Gabriel seemed slightly ashamed of it.

'So little happens here – they're like children,' he apologised.

But when the police contingent arrived at the conservatory and stared into the dead eyes of Henri Larche, they were brisk and efficient, courteous and patient, and all the things they should be. Curiously there was more of a 'hospital' feel to them than anything else. With low voices and sympathetic glances, the four policemen, photographer and doctor went through their paces in the narrow space around Henri's stiffening body.

'You don't have to watch all this,' muttered Gabriel.

'I'd rather.'

It was boiling hot in the conservatory with the sun high in a cloudless sky. Lebatre stood silently amongst the fleshy-leaved camellias at the back. He was a very fat man with a huge paunch somehow squeezed into a light grey suit. His face was as pouchy as his body and the perspiration stood out in little crystals on his forehead. The waiting seemed endless, and without speaking to Marius, Lebatre stood there and watched the solemn ritual until the police doctor pronounced himself finished. The doctor then muttered something to Gabriel and they went outside with inaudible excuses.

'Monsieur?'

'Yes?' Marius was watching a butterfly hovering on the mossy panes.

'Philippe Lebatre.'

They shook hands. Lebatre's palm was hot and dry.

'Is there somewhere we can talk?'

'Inside the house. It's cool in there.'

Lebatre smiled. It was a civilised, reflective smile and it gave an edge, a distinction to his pudgy appearance.

'Will you have him taken away?' Marius asked, looking down at his father.

'To the mortuary. Immediately, unless – '

'What?'

'You want to spend time with him.'

'No. You'd better take him away.'

They walked out into the harsh sunlight; Marius leading the way into the house with Lebatre a few paces behind him. We'll go to the study, he thought, wondering where Estelle had taken the old woman.

'Is this your father's room?'

'Yes,' Marius replied. Who else could it belong to? There could be no mistake. It was an old man's room. Cluttered and stuffy. The walls were thick with photographs and every surface seemed to leak dusty books and papers. A tall, solid oak bookcase took up an entire wall, crammed with Henri's law library. The books were jammed in higgledy-piggledy and there was dust on the glass. On a small table were dried flowers, bought from Marie and Mireille Leger's little shop. Next to them was a bottle of aperitif – St Raphael – and beside it were half a dozen clean shiny glasses.

'Can I offer you something?' asked Marius, seeing Lebatre's eyes on the label.

'Thank you.'

'Ice? I can fetch it.'

'Will that be a trouble?'

'A matter of seconds.'

'Thank you.'

Marius left him, his nugget eyes flitting round the room. Would Lebatre touch anything, he wondered, or was it just a visual inventory?

When he came back, the ice clinking in the two glasses, the mid-morning sun was casting dusty beams on to the dark-stained uncarpeted wooden floor. Marius poured the St Raphael on to the ice. He still felt very numb and the alcohol flooded him with a sense of well-being.

41

'A great tragedy,' said Lebatre respectfully.

Marius said nothing.

'Did you see your father at all this morning?'

'No. My mother woke me – to say he wasn't in the house.'

'Did she say where she thought he'd gone?'

'She said the Germans had taken him. My mother is suffering from the effects of a stroke. She is also very old. She lives in the past – or even not quite that.'

'I'm sorry.'

'It makes her happier than she would be otherwise.'

'Does she know he's dead?'

'Yes.'

'She thinks the Germans did it?' Lebatre's voice was gently understanding.

'She thought that then. But now she may have changed her mind. She has flashes of rationality.'

'So it was you who found him?'

'Yes.'

Lebatre paused, looking round at the dusty photographs. Then he said hesitantly: 'I am aware of the – pressures – surrounding him.'

'Who isn't, in this town?' snapped Marius.

'In a small town everything is news.'

'Yes. But St Esprit has only got one story.'

'The past is of great emotional importance here.' Lebatre paused. 'You are on vacation?'

'Officially. But I was spending the time trying to help my father clear his name.'

There was another short silence. Marius took another sip of the aperitif. The illogical feeling of well-being was gone; a sense of despair filled him. 'Do you think he could have killed himself?' he asked Lebatre, knowing he was asking a nonsensical question.

'No. It's possible that someone tried to make it look as if your father killed himself – in a rather half-hearted way. I would imagine that time was their problem. The doctor thinks he died somewhere around dawn.'

'Why should my father get up so early and go to the conservatory? In his pyjamas? If someone came to the house and lured him out there it would mean they opened the front

42

door and went up to his room. That would seem ludicrously risky. And I hardly think they threw stones up at his window. Unless there had been some kind of prior appointment? And why shouldn't he have told me in that case?'

'There's no sign of the door being forced,' replied Lebatre. 'Perhaps this person was well known to you. Someone who could come and go at will.'

'There's only Estelle, the girl who comes in from the village. She has a key. No one else could come and go like that – unless they found an unlatched window.'

'No one else at all?'

'Not that I know of. Visitors are pretty scarce at Letoric, particularly since the trial.'

'Has any evidence against him come to light?'

'None.' Marius cleared his throat. Despite the cool of the interior of the house, his shirt was sticking to him clammily. He looked at Lebatre's empty glass. 'Another?'

'Thank you.'

'You'll forgive me if I don't join you. You won't get any sense out of me if I do.' Marius slopped more St Raphael into Lebatre's glass.

'I could come back and ask – '

'Ask now.'

'Kummel is serving a life sentence,' stated Lebatre. 'Can't he clear your father's name?'

'We've already tried that.'

'How?'

'Through lawyers.'

'And?'

'He won't talk. He says he has nothing to say.'

'Does he *know*?'

Marius shrugged. 'He *must* have known.'

'Then why – ?'

'I can only suppose he's either mischievous – or he's too old to remember.'

There was a long silence. Then Lebatre said, 'Despite all that has happened, despite the fact that your father was surrounded by all kinds of possible enemies – is there anyone you know who might actually harm him?' He smiled nervously, as if he was asking a stupid question.

43

Marius shook his head. 'My parents have lived as recluses – ever since the trial.' Then he remembered. 'There were some abusive letters, written by one of the Leger sisters. Marie Leger. She imagined, quite erroneously, that my father had colluded with her brother Alain in disinheriting her and her sister Mireille. It's a very complicated business but I can assure you there was no truth in the accusations.'

'Do you have these letters?'

'He destroyed them.'

Lebatre sighed. 'Your father was a much accused man,' he said eventually.

'He suffered a good deal,' Marius replied.

'And his state of mind?' asked Lebatre in the gentle way he asked loaded questions that Marius was beginning to recognise – and to be wary of.

'He was worried – as you might well expect him to be.'

Lebatre nodded sympathetically. 'I gather your mother was in the Resistance – that she survived the Gestapo?'

'Yes. I'm very proud of her – and conscious of the irony as well.' He paused. 'The irony of the rumours surrounding my father,' he explained.

'Did you ever – have you ever believed him guilty?'

'No. It was not in my father to be as devious as that. To keep up the pretence of innocence, to show such bitterness about the accusations. And it would have been quite out of character for him to preside over some kangaroo court,' he added dismissively. But the familiar nagging thought returned. Did he really know his father?

'He hated the Nazis?'

'Of course.'

'Yet he carried on with his job?'

'It was a good front for my mother.'

'That was a conscious decision?'

'Of course.' Marius's voice was firm. 'We were never close but we did talk about that – and besides, Alain told me.'

'Alain?'

'Leger. He's the family lawyer – and my father's oldest friend. He was in the Resistance too. And is quite certain of my father's innocence.'

'These letters – ' began Lebatre.

The sweat broke out on Marius' forehead.

'Did you know the content?'

'Apparently they simply rambled on about the trial – and my father's alleged guilt.'

'That is all?'

'Yes.'

'Did you actually see them?'

'Never.'

Suppose he asked the Legers, thought Marius, blind panic coursing through him. Suppose they tell him about Jean-Pierre? Suppose he had to admit to the pathetic blackmail attempts? But what if he did, Marius tried to rationalise. A childhood experience? Mainly. Monique would be the first to understand. Slowly the panic drained out of him.

Another vehicle drove on to the weed-strewn gravel outside. Peering from one of the small, latticed windows, Marius could see that it was an ambulance.

'They're going to take him away,' said Lebatre quietly.

Marius turned away from the window and sat down abruptly.

'Would you like to see him go?'

Marius shook his head. 'Have you any more questions?' He saw again his father's blood – like a red lake around him. As if he was a stuck pig, drained and withered.

'A few.'

'Very well.'

'I'll be quick.'

Suddenly Marius wanted to prolong the interview, however dangerous it was. The longer Lebatre stayed, the longer he could put off seeing his mother.

'These letters from Marie Leger. How seriously did your father take them?'

'Not seriously at all. They constituted no threat.'

'When were they received?'

'Last Spring.'

'Did he receive any other letters? Any written threats?'

'Not to my knowledge.'

'Was he frightened?'

'Yes. He was also very angry. He didn't think I was doing enough.'

'And were you?'

'No. I couldn't. I was frightened of what I might unearth.' He paused, realising he was contradicting himself, betraying doubts about his father's innocence. 'I only ran through the motions just to satisfy him – which it didn't. I realise I was prevaricating,' he added rather lamely.

'Does Commissaire Rodiet know of any positive evidence against your father?'

'Not as far as I know.'

'This – incident – in the war. What exactly happened?'

'It was in 1944. A German officer was murdered – and half a dozen young people were executed in revenge.'

'And Rodiet's mother?'

'She tried to intervene.'

Lebatre was silent. Then he said: 'Commissaire Rodiet was in the Resistance himself. He'll know more.'

Marius shrugged. 'Perhaps he does.' There was another long uncomfortable silence.

'Are there any more questions?' asked Marius abruptly.

'No. Not for now. I don't need to say that you shouldn't talk to the press.'

'Of course not.'

'Don't get involved professionally.' Lebatre's voice was prim.

'How can I *not* get involved?' snapped Marius. What the hell did the man expect him to do? Detach himself from the whole affair?

'I'm very sorry about what has happened,' said Lebatre with the empty ring of official condolence.

'Thank you.'

Lebatre got heavily to his feet, putting his glass down carefully on a little rafia mat. He looked out of the window. 'Commissaire Rodiet is coming across.'

'He'll find his way in.'

'Goodbye, monsieur. I'll ring you later.' Lebatre walked out, his enormous frame still retaining dignity. Marius tried not to listen to his whispered exchange with Gabriel in the hall. Then Gabriel came in.

'Did Lebatre handle it?'

'Carefully.'

'They're taking your father away.'

'I know. I don't want to go out there.'

Gabriel nodded. Then he said, 'They're still dusting for fingerprints in the conservatory – it'll be a while yet.'

'I must go to my mother.'

'Anything I can do?'

Marius shook his head. 'There must have been a lot of people who hated him.' His voice was flat.

Rodiet shrugged. 'Gossip doesn't necessarily imply intense hatred.'

'But there *is* someone who hated enough,' replied Marius.

André phoned Annette from the office. She stood in the bedroom of the tall house overlooking the plane trees, imagining him sitting on the swivel chair behind the large empty desk, the computer screen in front of him, the faint hum of the newsroom behind the heavy partitions.

'What are you doing?' he asked.

'Looking out on the trees, watching old Madame Pelier walking across to the café.'

'What's the time?'

'It's two. I was going to have a siesta.' She had felt particularly depressed about their relationship today.

'I've had some news. Henri's dead.'

'What?' Annette found it hard to register what he was saying.

'Henri. He's dead.'

She sat down on the bed, shaking, the sweat clammy on her body. Shock waves filled her; everything else was driven out of her head.

'Are you all right?' He seemed very concerned.

'I'm all right.' But she was wondering if she was going to be sick.

'He was murdered.'

'Yes.' Her voice was emotionless but her stomach churned.

'You don't sound surprised.'

'Are you?'

'I don't know – I suppose I never expected anyone to do it, in the end.'

'Why not?' Her voice trembled.

'I never thought he was hated *enough*. Now I feel partly responsible.'

47

'Don't be so feeble.' Her voice was hard, contemptuous. 'If you can't take the consequences you shouldn't have printed that piece.' But all the time she was thinking, Henri dead at last? She still couldn't believe it. Annette stared out of the window, anxious to touch normality, but the street looked oddly out of true. Perhaps it was the hard early afternoon sunlight that made the distortion. Henri murdered? Killed by the *Journal*, more likely.

'His throat was cut.' He sounded more authoritative now.

'Who found him?'

'Larche. Marius Larche. In the conservatory. Rodiet says the police are "pursuing their enquiries", as they say.'

'Anything else?'

'The place was wiped clean of fingerprints.'

'So it's quite a professional job?'

'Not exactly. A clumsy attempt was made to make it look as if he had committed suicide.'

'Will you be home late?'

'Yes. I've got to put this together – see if there's anything else we can find out.'

'That story', she said flatly, 'will run and run.'

His voice was more confident as he said goodbye and rang off.

Annette walked to the window. She felt calmer now, and when she looked out into the street, the plane trees, the stone benches on the paved area in the middle, the wilting flowers, the empty café tables, the urinoir – all were normal. But now it was as if sound had been removed. The whole street was relentlessly silent. She hardly dared breathe as she stared out at the desolation, listening to Henri's voice:

'You'll leave.'

'Leave?'

'Get out.'

Annette remembered Henri's words exactly as she continued to gaze down at the bleached-out street.

'But why? I'm doing a good job.'

They were in the cluttered study; she could see Henri's livid, working face. There was a smell of dried flowers in the air.

'You shouldn't have opened the letter.'

'I always open your correspondence.'

48

'That was personal.'

Annette shook her head as she had shaken it then. What did the old fool mean? He had been writing a kind of memoir and she had been checking it for him. At first it had been pleasant to work in the crumbling château. She had been bored and the opportunity to work with a suspected collaborator had appealed to the curiosity in her. Life with André had been better then, but she had needed an occupation. Since their marriage she had taken care not to accept his offer of a job on the newspaper.

Annette had been brought up in Paris, the only child of a rich property developer who had converted a number of old studios into studio apartments of immense size, style and vogue. They were sold at vast profit and, as a matter of course, Annette went to a school in Switzerland on some of the proceeds and then to the Sorbonne where she had met André. Later she had become a secretary to the editor of *Paris Soir* while André joined *Le Figaro* as a junior reporter. A year later they married and she watched him change jobs and loyalties with amazing speed until the *Journal* post came up in Aix. Giving up her work, hoping for children, she moved with him. The work with Henri had been a panacea.

'Get out!' She heard his voice again as she looked down at the still-silent street.

'I don't understand.' She had been close to tears.

'You shouldn't have opened it.' He sounded childish and resentful.

'I'm sorry – I didn't read anything.' But of course she had and Henri had known she had.

'I'm not trying to clear my name,' he had told her when she had first been employed. The Lyon trial was over then by three years. 'I'm merely trying to bring a sense of order into my life. I'm going to write a memoir of my war experiences – just as they happened. I've kept diaries – those I would like you to check and type up.'

So – the old lady had accused him. *Didier knows*, she had written. *Didier knows you killed them*. She had been disturbed by the bitterness of Marie Leger's writing, but she had no idea who Didier was – and she had not read on. She felt sorry for her – and for the tired old man.

'You couldn't contain your curiosity, could you?' he had

sneered at her, but his eyes weren't challenging. They were terrified. Was his agitation due to Didier? Or was it the fact that Marie's vitriol had also included allegations about Marius Larche's homosexual affair? *Screwing*, she had scrawled. *Unnatural screwing*. Then Henri told her again to get out – and this time she went. But when she arrived home, something prevented her telling André. Perhaps she pitied the old man. Perhaps she didn't trust André's nose for a story. Either way, she kept quiet, putting her departure down to a trivial disagreement and gathering boredom. He believed her.

Now, Annette looked at her watch. Three o'clock already. She must have been staring out of the window musing for nearly an hour. She would have to go to the restaurant soon. But still she lingered, wondering, waiting. Thinking of Henri. Thinking of his murderer. Thinking of the letter and its poisonous abuse. Didier. Screwing. Somehow she felt contaminated.

Alain was walking in the forest that connected Ste Michelle with Letoric. The afternoon light filtered through the pine trees into light golden patches on the hard earth. He smelt dry, sandy soil, and wafting up on the light wind, the fragrance of the lavender fields below him. Alain had walked up the hill into the pines wanting to think of his dead friend, to put time and space around him.

They had often walked up here, through the sun-drenched lavender, into the cool, dusty shade of the pines. From here he could see the crouched town with its orderly avenues and deserted central square. Siesta time. A car crawled towards the tennis courts, a burst of music blared from behind closed shutters and was as abruptly silenced. The whole somnolent afternoon in the timeless streets seemed light years away from him. He was up here in a different world. With Henri.

This was their favourite place, particularly since they had both retired. Alain was a widower – Hélène had died ten years ago with a quick forgiving cancer that had taken her away in weeks. They had one daughter, Gaby, who was an accountant in Paris. Ste Michelle was large, roomy, well cared for, with ornamental gardens and a fountain whose cherubs, unlike those at Letoric, gushed water from practically every orifice. But it was run by the servants – a middle-aged cook-housekeeper and her chauffeur husband who served him his meals but were unable to keep him company. So, Henri had been family in a way. They saw each other most days – for a drink, for chess, occasionally for dinner and regularly, usually each Sunday afternoon, for a walk amongst the trees on the parched hill.

They had known each other from childhood. Alain was a little older, more extrovert, a keen sportsman who had, over the years, taken on the role of protector to the younger, more bookish Henri. Their families had been close. There had been parties and tennis and boules and hunting for wild boar. Then there had been marriage and the birth of their children – Marius and Gaby. As a child she had been outgoing and full of vitality – the very opposite of Marius, who was introverted, moody, given to fits of passion.

Alain knew the boy was close to his mother – that Henri was remote for him. They had talked about it many times. Henri had minded, had wanted to reach him. But saw no way of doing so.

'He shuts himself away – keeps me out,' he had told Alain when Marius was about eleven. 'I can't get near him. It's my fault – I neglected him while he was growing up. Damn my career – that's what's done it. My own selfishness.'

Throughout the occupation, Alain and Solange had grown close as they ostensibly functioned as innocent civilians by day – and saboteurs by night. It had been a heady existence, planning, intriguing, carrying out the wrecking of German communications. There had been about twelve of them, including the young boys Didier and Gabriel, working in the foothills, smuggling arms and explosives, relatively unchanged by the occupation. He had once wanted to make love to Solange, but she had gently refused and after that he didn't ask her again. She had been so beautiful, so daring in her successful clandestine operations. Then towards the end of the occupation she had had Marius – and her work for the Maquis had ceased. From then on, Alain had seen her only occasionally, socially, and he received the unspoken message that she wanted to keep him at a safe distance.

Alain often looked back to the war which had been such a central focus of everyone's lives and their work with the

Resistance which had been so vital. To this day he still remembered the exact location of the clandestine meetings on this very hill, and the cache of weapons and explosives behind a partition in the cellars of Letoric that the Gestapo had never found despite their frequent random searches. He had risked his life every week and so had Solange but Henri had remained detached.

'I would be too much of a threat,' he had said, justifying his lack of involvement. 'If they suspected me, they would soon start suspecting all of you.'

Alain had never questioned the logic of this at the time, but now he had to acknowledge that it was simply that Henri was too selfish and too timorous as well.

Then there was Didier. Occasionally Alain went to see him and very occasionally Didier recognised him. But most of the time he was locked up in his own self-created world: the only place he could inhabit now – although Alain considered him institutionalised rather than mad.

As he walked to the brow of the hill, he felt desperately, unbearably alone. Then he saw the man, standing just underneath the brow of the hill, sitting on a grassy outcrop, staring down at Letoric. He instantly recognised him. Jean-Pierre Claude – the farm labourer who lived with his mother in the old cottage near the end of the weed-tangled Letoric drive. What did he want, wondered Alain indignantly, forcing his limbs into a more hurried stride. He must know he was trespassing – and trespassing to Alain was a major crime. The Ste Michelle estate was his own world, and he believed passionately in the privacy of his own property – the place he had even wrested away from his own sisters who he had known would only mismanage it. To have seen Ste Michelle divided into three shares would have been intolerable, and besides, he knew that they would be tempted to sell some of it as building land. To Alain, his family home and its land was sacred and he would fight to the bitter end to protect every inch of it.

4

The old man suddenly came into view. He was tall and gaunt, impressive despite his slight stoop, with a full head of startlingly white hair and a white moustache. Jean-Pierre had always admired his looks. Landowner Leger, brother of the two old girls, a recluse who was said to have been a Resistance hero, and who now was so passionate about his deep love for his own particular patch of native land. There had been some kind of dispute with his sisters over the estate and they didn't speak. Jean-Pierre knew he was trespassing, but he often did and had rarely seen anyone here at the top of the hill. He wanted to look at Letoric – the scene of the crime – and perhaps catch a sight of Marius. For a long time now, Jean-Pierre had been obsessed with him. It seemed like a lifetime since Jean-Pierre had seduced him as a young man, mostly for the fun of having the local toff. Recently the obsession had grown deeper, and lately he had thought of him every day – the days that stretched into eternity – a life sentence of toiling on the land. Meanwhile Marius Larche had his rich professional life; a high ranking policemen who might care about the past enough to part with some money. After all, he was up to his neck in scandal already. Surely he didn't want any more. The money, and with it the chance of escaping a life in the fields, were only what he deserved.

Sometimes he went for a weekend in Lyon where he could make money as a prostitute. He knew his way around, knew what to give and what to receive. But he was in his forties now and the drink and his mother's generous food had ruined his figure. The bastard owes me, he thought. And with Henri dead, maybe Marius would be more vulnerable.

53

'You realise you are trespassing?'

Jean-Pierre looked up, purposely vague. 'Sorry?'

'You're trespassing.'

'I didn't know.'

'You know now.'

Jean-Pierre got slowly to his feet. 'I was having a look at the house. The old man was killed this morning.'

'Leave them alone.'

'Who do you think did it?'

'Just get off my land.' Alain advanced threateningly on him but Jean-Pierre stood his ground.

'They killed him for what they thought he did, didn't they? All those rumours – they got him in the end.'

'If you don't go I shall call the police.'

'You were friends, weren't you? You and him?'

Alain turned on his heel. 'I'll go and ring them now. Give them your description.'

'No need. I'm going.'

'And don't let me ever see you here again.'

Jean-Pierre winked at him and began to walk away.

'Mother?'

'She's got herself in a state.' Estelle was standing in the darkened bedroom by the window. His mother lay on the bed. There was a curious smell in the room – part human sweat, part perfume. Then he realised something. Estelle had been splashing on his mother's eau-de-Cologne.

'Mother?'

She was bathed in sweat, lying on the counterpane, rocking herself slowly to and fro.

Marius took her shoulders and tried to comfort her by holding them down with both his hands. Her eyes were closed and her lips were scaly. She had been beautiful once, he reminded himself. Beautiful and intelligent. And brave. His friend. Then she opened her eyes and looked up at him.

'Marius.'

'Yes?'

'Stay with me.'

'Of course.'

54

'That girl. Why do we keep her? She's such a slut. But she's kind to me.'

'No one else will come,' he said woodenly, realising that she had arrived at one of her rare calm, clear moods when the clouds had temporarily lifted. How long did they have, he wondered.

'Why?' she asked, her genuine innocence momentarily appealing.

'They won't come because of Father. Because of – what they say about him.'

'He never collaborated. I should know that. To be honest, he would never have taken that risk. Your father was not a man for taking risks.'

A wave of hope and of something else that he couldn't immediately identify swept over Marius. Was it reassurance, he wondered.

'Where is he?' she asked.

'He's dead.'

'His heart?' Her voice was gentle and soft, not rasping as it so often was nowadays.

'No.' He took her hands and kissed them. 'Someone – someone killed him.'

'Who?' She didn't seem shocked.

'I don't know. The police are on to it.'

'Gabriel?' She laughed. 'Him?' The laugh rang hollowly in Marius's ears.

'There's someone else – '

'And Henri? Did he suffer?'

'No.'

'That's good. It was bound to happen. Poor Henri.' Her eyes clouded and he knew he was beginning to lose her again.

'Mother, do you know who did it?'

'The Boche.'

'No. It wasn't.'

'Then who?' She moved her head restlessly from side to side.

'Can you think who would have done it?'

'The rumours made him enemies.'

'But do you know *who* – who was his *worst* enemy?'

'Yes.'

'Mother – '

'I know.'

'Tell me who – ' The tension was unbearable. Suddenly he was convinced that she *did* know.

'It's always been on the cards.'

'*Who*?'

'But once they arrived – '

'*Who* arrived?'

'The Boche.' She began to rock again. 'He was a brave man. A good man. He wouldn't give in to them. So they killed him. Poor Henri.' The rocking became a little faster. 'Henri – '

'Mother, we're talking about one person. *Not* the Germans. Someone now. They called him away this morning. He went with them, or met them. By arrangement, or something. Someone he *knew*.'

'They came in here. Looking.'

'Mother – '

'They took me away. They hurt me. Hurt me badly. Henri – '

'It's Marius.'

'Henri. Stay close. Touch me.'

'It's *Marius*, Mother.'

'Come in beside me.'

'Excuse me.'

Marius glanced up. Dr Lucas stood on the threshold. Immediately behind him was Gabriel.

'I'm glad you've come,' said Marius, getting off the bed and walking towards him. 'She's been clear for a little while. Now she's babbling again.'

The doctor nodded. 'That will happen.'

'Did she say anything of note?' asked Gabriel urgently.

'She says she knows who killed him,' said Marius drily.

'Who?' Gabriel's voice was sharp.

'The Boche. The Germans,' he replied wearily.

'She'll rest now.'

'Thank you.'

Dr Lucas paused. 'I'm putting her on stronger sedatives. It would be as well – to administer the dose yourself.' He was a little man, hesitant and anxious to cover himself.

'Yes, I will.'

'Good – very good. Call me if you need me again.' He scuttled past like a frightened rabbit.

'Do you want me to stay?' said Gabriel.

Marius looked at his watch. It was nearly five. 'I don't know what to do next,' he confessed.

'Do nothing. Have a drink.'

'I'm uneasy about – '

'Go on. Have one.'

Once again they stood in Henri's cramped and dusty study. This time he poured them whisky.

'How's the investigation going?' he asked.

'Proceeding.'

'You don't know anything?'

'Nothing.'

'Is Lebatre good?'

'Solid. Very solid. Deeply conscientious.'

'Any theories yourself?'

'Yes. It seems possible that your father was killed to prevent him telling something he knew – something incriminating.'

'So you're saying the motive wasn't necessarily revenge.'

'I'm saying we mustn't be blinkered.'

Marius drank more whisky. Then he made a decision. 'Could I ask a few questions?'

'Go ahead.'

'Gabriel – your mother was killed – you have every reason to hate.'

'You are regarding me as a suspect?' Gabriel gave him a mocking, almost querulous smile.

'Don't be a fool – '

'But you should. Lebatre must question me. I do have a very good motive.'

'How have you stayed so open-minded all this time?'

'Perhaps because I never loved my mother. She was a domineering, interfering woman and she made my father's life hell.'

Marius looked at Gabriel intently. 'I didn't – '

'No. I haven't said any of this before. But that is why I have been so even-handed – in case you hadn't noticed.' He laughed. 'I was seventeen when she was killed, yet her death filled me with relief. All the way through my adolescence she had

57

tormented and bullied me. Now I understand that she wanted me to stand up to her. And when I wouldn't, I think she loathed me – had such enormous contempt for me.' He paused. 'As you know my father was gentle. He and I spent years of happiness after her death. I thanked the Germans for it. Of course I made a show of grief – even at that age I was conscious of the need for self-dramatisation. But really I was glad. I was in the Maquis – I knew she did a brave thing. But I had nothing to do with those young men or their execution.' His voice was very firm.

'And your father?'

'He had nothing to do with the Resistance; he was too busy with his work as a country doctor. Mother's death – and the nature of it – was not something we discussed.'

'Thank you for telling me.'

Gabriel frowned. 'I'm not saying she wasn't a brave woman,' he repeated. 'She would have died defending us. Instead she died defending them.'

'What exactly happened?'

'I'll tell you. But let me tell you something else first.' He drank more whisky. Outside a bird called. A dog was barking in the distance. 'As I said, we mustn't be blinkered and there could be another motive for your father's murder, but frankly I have a gut-feeling that if we want to find out who killed your father we have to go back to that day in early May when they took those boys out to the field and killed them.'

'You mean their relations – their parents – '

'We would need to eliminate them from our enquiries.'

'Lebatre – '

'He's already checking them.'

'I see. You were going to say – '

'Mother? She had a close friend – Chantal Relais. One of the Relais sons was taken. Mother hurried to the spot and remonstrated. Naturally they didn't listen to her. But she persisted – even to the point of standing in the firing line.'

Marius gasped, staring at Gabriel in amazement.

'Yes. She was an exceptionally brave woman. And as I said – an exceptionally domineering one. She nagged the German soldiers like she nagged us. I believe they tried to turn her away.' He paused. 'Then Mother stood in the firing line – so

58

they shot her as they shot the others. She's buried in the churchyard. Down there. Near where they'll bury your father.'

'Thank you for telling me all this.' Marius stared out at the dusk outside. The cicadas were beginning. It was a sound that usually comforted him. Now he was finding it oppressive.

'You are owed the explanation.'

'I think I'll take a walk.'

'Where?'

'To the field.'

'Do you want company?'

'No. Do you mind?'

Gabriel shook his head. 'Of course not. But I *shall* mind if you involve yourself professionally.'

'I won't do that.'

'No?'

For the first time Marius could feel Gabriel's hostility. 'No.'

'Why don't you go back to Lyon?'

'Are you mad? What about my mother?' Marius was more bewildered than indignant.

'Isn't this the time to have her put away – for her own good?'

'I think that's for me to decide.' Marius was angry now. 'And there are the funeral arrangements.'

'They'll take a few days,' he agreed. 'Those and the arrangements about your mother. Then you should go. You can do no good here. Leave it to us.'

'I'll think about it.'

'Are you angry?'

But the anger had gone. Marius just felt punch-drunk.

'No.'

'I'm trying to think of her own good – and yours.'

'I know.'

'I'd better go.' Gabriel drained his whisky. He was looking anxious now and Marius felt an urgent need to reassure him.

'Don't worry. You may be right. But I have to think.'

'Is Estelle still here?'

'Yes. She's good with Mother in her rough way.

'She's a slut.'

'A useful one.' There was an awkward silence. 'I suppose I should phone the undertaker,' said Marius suddenly.

'Not until the coroner releases the body.' Gabriel stood up. He touched Marius's shoulder. 'Take care.' He withdrew, a grey shadow in the evening glow.

5

The light was fading fast as Marius made his way down the overgrown track that had originally been the formal drive to the Château Letoric. The sense of loss was growing in him – an empty ache in the pit of his stomach. Maybe Gabriel was right in his domineering way. Domineering? He laughed out loud and stopped, surprised at the sound. He was like his mother then. Just the same, perhaps. How ironic. But even so, it was a temptation to go back to Monique. He should have phoned her. To go back to Monique would be in the nature of a great escape. Evading the repercussions of his father's death, his mother's plight and, of course, Jean-Pierre Claude.

As he walked, Marius thought of his mother – and of how she had been before the stroke. Of course he had been a mother's boy – no doubt of that – and he had been very conscious of how desperately his father had tried to reach him. But he had resisted – and eventually Henri had gone away, defeated. After that, Marius knew that his father would no longer trespass into the special space he and his mother inhabited. It was not that Marius hated him, it was just that there was no place for him. His mother was everything. Too young to understand the full implications of the Maquis, for a long time he only dimly realised how brave she had been, especially when interrogated, as the Provençal years rolled slowly by. Even when he was older, Marius had not wanted to think about the danger in the mountains. Indeed for years he had been terrified of the rocky promontories, seeing against the pine trees and the shale the dark shadows of Nazi uniforms as they pursued his mother further and further up the boulder-strewn paths. All he wanted was the warm immediacy of his post-war mother with all her light-hearted, teasing affection and their shared walks across the fields. He had been desperately in love with her, wanting only her company, never the detached masculinity of his father.

He remembered a picnic amongst the pine trees on the lower slopes of the mountains. Her gaze had travelled up to the scree and to a cave where she had once told him that she 'and Uncle Alain and Gabriel had hidden all one night while the Nazis combed the slopes'. He had not wanted to know, and had deliberately looked away, down to the heat-hazed fields where a young boy worked with his bully of a father. From thence he was glad to catch sight of the boy, to watch his muscular shoulders, to see the sweat glistening on his bare back. It had been some time before he met Jean-Pierre on a solitary walk along the side of the lavender fields – some time before the boy took him in his arms in the gardens of the château.

From where he was walking, Marius could see the church spire and some of the roofs of the town. They were hazy and insubstantial, like the mental picture of his father's murder. He had left his mother with Estelle, still rambling, the brief clarity glimmered away. But his conversation with Estelle had been provocative, although she had volunteered what he needed very quickly.

'Monsieur will need me tonight?'

'Sorry?'

'The old lady has had a bad shock. She shouldn't be left.'

'I shall be with her.'

'It's such a burden for you, Monsieur. I would be very willing to stay, to help. Of course I would need some small – '

'Yes, of course you will. Well, perhaps you had better stay. I can't be here all the time. I have arrangements to make.'

'The funeral?'

'Yes, and – er – others.'

'You will be investigating the murder, monsieur?'

Damn her blatant curiosity, he had thought. He had looked at her tarty, dirty clothes and inwardly cursed. But she was all he had. And Estelle did seem to have a way with the old lady. Swiftly he had come to a generous financial arrangement with her. But soon she was quietly repeating the question: 'You are investigating?'

'Of course not. That's up to the local police.'

She had lowered her eyes. 'But you have more experience, monsieur. You are in Interpol.'

Somehow he had shut her up. Now he was in the valley, walking towards the stile that led to the field where they died. Sunflowers nodded in the light, honeysuckle-scented evening breeze that brought blessed relief from the heat. He looked back at the house. At least two of the shutters were hanging loose, cracked and with paint peeling. In his childhood his father had ordered the servants to close the shutters – all twenty pairs of them – each night. To keep out prying eyes. Strangers' eyes. There was another smell from the hill. Pine needles, he thought. Would they have smelt them, all those years ago? Lined up in the field of execution. He pictured Madame Rodiet, flinging herself between the prisoners and their executioners – and going down in a hail of bullets.

Marius climbed the stile. The field was high with corn. Was it growing the crop then? Were they pushed into the centre, trampling the rustling stalks, their blood staining the ears of wheat rusty red? Or was it just grass and they stood starkly against the sun, waiting to be mowed down, maybe not even understanding why they were there? And were there eyes watching from the edge of the field? Parents. Relatives. Brothers. Sisters. Eyes that were recording the scene, imprinting it in their hearts for ever – until the day would come when revenge could be taken. And against his will, Marius saw his father's figure walking stiffly into the field, very erect, very dignified, his expression inscrutable. So intense was the image that he could see him now, indistinct in his dark suit against the corn. Then the figure moved and began to limp towards him, calling his name.

'Marius.'

He froze.

Alain. He had looked so like his father. But thank God, it was definitely Alain, looking as distinguished as ever and now embracing him.

'Marius.'

'It's good to see you.'

'I'm not intruding?' If ever the expression grief-stricken had been used to good purpose it was now. The suffering was deeply etched on Alain's rugged features.

They walked along the lee of the field and then began to climb. Clumps of rock gleamed dully in the twilight while the steady beat of the cicadas seemed to increase.

'I can't believe it,' said Alain, panting a little.

'Nor me.'

'A world without Henri – it's unbelievable.'

'You were very close.' Marius fell in with the emotion of the conversation easily. It was what he needed. A catharsis.

'Close enough for me to know that he would never have presided over such a court. He wasn't strong enough; I'd always protected him, but I couldn't have averted this.' He was still panting a little as he walked, but as if it was the anguish that was exhausting him, not the mountain path.

Marius said nothing, but looked up the rocky hill. On its promontory lay the ruins of a small church. His father had once climbed up there with him when he was a child and together they had watched the twilight gather round the valley, deep shadows lengthening on the rocks until all was dark and the tiny lights of St Esprit gleamed up at them like fire-flies. It was one of the few times when they were alone together – one of the few times he had not resented his father's presence. He could remember sounds, the banging of doors, the revving of a car engine, a dog barking. Yet all these were like the mutterings from some alien planet, light years away from their rocky, ecclesiastical eyrie. His earliest memories of his father were his remoteness, his preoccupation as he walked around the formal gardens of Letoric, admonishing and advising. Of course they had kissed, but the kisses always seemed cold and distanced – little ice-drops expelled from his father's dry lips. Yet he knew his father loved him, but in a locked-in way. He was never able to reach into Marius' life, or to have any understanding of him.

His mother on the other hand continuously produced all kinds of surprises, some good, some not so good – like tennis with the overtly competitive Feynols or chess with the ever-vigilant Hortense Descartes, though fortunately she gradually began to avoid the company of Hélène and Gaby Leger. But the good things – picnics and outings, holidays (usually taken without his father), cinema and theatre – were memorable and always worthy of the anticipation, unlike so many other aspects of life. The driving force in his mother was the only aspect of her that Marius found threatening; he was conscious of being swept along, not so much in her wake, but in front of her, with his mother a giant bellows behind him. When he was a child, Marius allowed himself to be pumped ahead, protecting himself with books and daydreams. But as puberty brought a miserable self-consciousness, Marius became prickly, suspecting insults, accepting an imagined inferiority. By this stage he was regularly seeing Jean-Pierre, their clandestine meetings reminding him of the unwillingly realised days of his mother's work in the Maquis. He and Jean-Pierre went to considerable pains not to be seen, and they met in obscure parts of the pine woods or in a barn. As a result, he grew withdrawn and afraid and in the holidays he roamed restlessly around Letoric, dwarfed by his inhibitions, observed by Jean-Pierre, flaring up at times, resisting proffered and fabricated friendship until he went to university. Schooldays in Lyon had been different, for here Marius had made friendships that he would never bring home. Close, passionate, formed with either sex but never with a sexual result. It had been only Jean-Pierre whom he had gone to over the years, but Jean-Pierre had seemed – a non-person? Someone of no consequence? Someone who did not exist in his life? None of the descriptions were quite right. He turned to Alain, suddenly needing to reach up out of the deadly maw of the past. They had walked on, almost up to the ruined church, and he had not been aware of it. They had climbed in companionable silence, but in the back of his mind Marius was all too well aware that, like his father, Alain was something of a stranger.

'Gabriel wants me to go back to Lyon.'

'I can see why.'

'Professional jealousy?'

'I wouldn't put it as strongly as that.' Until now he hadn't considered the possibility.

'But he'll want to question you.'

'Maybe he thinks he can do it better in Lyon.'

'Perhaps you should go,' said Alain gently. 'Your friend . . .'

Last winter when Monique had visited Letoric with him Alain had come over to dine with them. Marius had been grateful for his presence. Somehow both his parents had seemed livelier, less depressing while he was there.

'Monique? It will be good to see her.'

But would it? Suddenly Marius had the desperate desire to stay at Letoric to see it all through. They walked on in companionable silence.

During his university days at the Sorbonne and later at the Lyon law school Marius emerged from the confines of his childhood and adolescence. He made friends, enjoyed sex with women and headed vigorously towards a successful law degree. He consumed music and painting and literature with a raw, insatiable appetite. It was as if he had truly come alive for the first time. Then he met Natasha. She was partly Russian, and he became as obsessed with her as he had been with Jean-Pierre. She also was studying law, but unlike Marius' other friends she took it all rather lightly, with only the vaguest idea of the future, apparently regarding law school as a haven. She seemed to want to fail, to retake, to stay on longer. Marius found out why. Natasha's father had been having an affair, and just before she entered the law school her mother had committed suicide. Natasha's world was shattered. She had been devoted to her mother and greatly admired her mother's Russian passion – the passion that made her go on consuming aspirin until she was certain that any attempt to save her life with a stomach pump would be quite useless.

Once she had confided in him, they grew even closer, and for a year Marius was ecstatically happy. He forgot his background, evaded the night-time allure of what Jean-Pierre had to offer. Life with Natasha was complete. They hardly ever saw anyone else and depended on each other totally. She was – or had become – a strange mixture of vulnerability, sudden enthusiasms – and abject fear. To be her protector provided Marius with the greatest emotional fulfilment.

Then, one evening, they arranged to meet at a restaurant near the river-bank. She had wanted to buy some books at a small bookshop nearby and Marius had a late tutorial. It was February and the darkness at nine was bitter black. She didn't arrive. Marius searched for her everywhere – and then went to the police. A day later Natasha was washed up on a beach a mile or so down the Rhône. At first his numbed mind had leapt to suicide – like her mother. But the police told him she had been raped and battered to death. They told him not to see her but he insisted, and as Marius stared down at the bloated suet whiteness of her body and the misshapen thing that had once been her head, something broke inside him. That summer he left law school and joined the Lyon Police Department. They were keen to have a recruit of his calibre and, after a graduate training course, he filtered round various departments until, much later, he joined Interpol. Over the intervening years he mourned for Natasha, and the grief intensified rather than lessened as time passed. He became the shell of a personality; ten years elapsed before he felt he was becoming human again. And during that time, off and on, he had returned to the sexual comfort of Jean-Pierre. Not that this had blunted his pain, but gradually it was as if he had absorbed Natasha in some shallow pit inside him. She was a part of him. And in his career he was avenging her. Promoted to Detective Chief Inspector, Marius was good. He had a high success rate, and his investigations were always methodical, sometimes visionary. At Letoric, his mother – and no doubt his father – were very proud of him. But still it was only his mother's attention he craved and he managed to squeeze in time with her at Letoric. Not much, but enough to reassure him that she had the same driving force as before. She had joined a women's club in St Esprit and had become immersed in trying to keep up the Letoric gardens on her own. She hated gardeners – only wanted her own sense of creation and order. At the same time she was growing closer to his father and the two, now in their seventies, were becoming dependent on each other. Then his father retired. Six months later Wolfgang Kummel went on trial in Lyon and the persecution began. At first his mother was vigorously supportive. Then she had the stroke.

'Shall we stop at the church?' asked Alain.

'It's where I used to sit with Father.'

'Then perhaps – '

'No. I'd like to.'

Alain hesitated and then sat down. Marius settled down beside him. The lights winked back.

'I liked Monique,' he said, 'but didn't really get a chance to talk to her properly.'

'It was a good evening. I was grateful to you.'

'Will you bring her down again?'

'Yes – yes, of course I will.'

'Did you meet on a case?'

Marius laughed. It felt as if he had not done so in years. 'No. I met her at dinner with some mutual friends. An inspector in Lyon. She is a friend of his wife's. A conventional introduction.'

'And she's a historian?'

'At the university in Lyon.'

'Has she been married?'

'Yes. She's divorced,' said Marius briefly. He was surprised at Alain's curiosity. He had always seemed so detached. In his childhood Marius had always thought of him as rather glamorous – a Frenchman from a bygone age, with a love of wine and cheese, of the classic life, of belching grandly without covering his mouth. A wealthy lawyer of the old school with a dead wife whom Marius could hardly remember – and a sophisticated daughter whom he had been frightened of and was now vaguely curious to see. But she rarely came home and Marius had wondered if there was an estrangement.

'Why was it necessary for you to protect my father?' asked Marius suddenly, the thought surfacing, ready to be aired and discussed. It was curiosity, he supposed, rather than anything else.

'He lacked confidence.' Alain spoke slowly. 'We'd been friends and neighbours for a very long time. We'd seen much trouble together – and discussed it on our walks. He was a good man. Not a collaborator. I would never believe that. After Klaus Barbie we French have become obsessed with the problem – what is collaboration?' He paused. Alain was looking down at the field where they had been shot, the texture of which was rapidly disappearing into the night. 'Marshal Pétain was our symbol of collaboration, but what people don't realise is that it was a French proposal that Germany and France should be equal partners in government, not a German demand. Of course Hitler entirely rejected the idea . . .' He turned to look at Marius. 'Your father would have nothing to do with the Movement – particularly as your mother had everything to do with it. He knew he would endanger it; as an eminent judge he would be too much in the public eye. And this question of him working with the Nazis, well, he was also working for the French government, so you can't call that collaboration. As for presiding over a kangaroo court, he would never even have contemplated it. Still you know all this . . .' His voice trailed away.

'On that day – when the young people were taken out into that field and shot – did you talk it over with him?'

'We were really horrified. It was absolutely appalling. Both Henri and I felt so powerless. We registered the strongest possible objection to the local commandant. But of course – it was out of our hands.' He paused, watching Marius closely. 'I could have told you all this – at any time since you arrived from Lyon, or at any time before that. Why are you asking me now?' Marius said nothing and Alain continued. 'Is it because you were afraid to ask? That I might have something to tell you?'

'I was going to start asking questions. But I procrastinated too much.'

'Your father wanted to clear his name.' There was a trace of impatience in Alain's tone.

'Yes – but I couldn't face finding him guilty,' said Marius. 'Do you blame me?' he asked with sudden anguish.

'No – I might well have done the same thing. If you love them then there's a resistance to digging deep. The pain of feeling other people's hatred.' Alain shivered and stood up. 'It's growing cold up here. Shall we walk back?'

Again they walked in the silence Marius would closely associate with that evening. The pungent scents of the mountainside suffused him as they edged down and he thought of Monique, suddenly needing her desperately. It would be good to take their advice and go to Lyon. She would be sympathetic, attentive, yet give him space. She would be perfect. Little stones rattled under his feet and a rabbit scampered across a dry gully below them.

Their second meeting had been at an antique book fair. Marius had wanted some of the Letoric books revalued, not with a view to selling but to reinsuring. He had taken a couple of early editions of Victor Hugo to the Lyon sale to consult one of the experts.

Monique had been there on a similar errand: an aunt was about to sell part of her library and, being infirm, had entrusted her niece with the task. They had met again at one of the stands, and while their books were being valued, had found each other attractive. She was tall, willowy, a few years younger than he with a long oval face that elegantly – and eloquently – displayed the driest of dry humour. An historian, she special-ised in the First World War and had already written a couple of books on the Somme and Flanders fields. Now with her fellowship at Lyon, she was only meant to give a few lectures. The main purpose of her appointment was to allow her to concentrate on a paper she was writing about Ypres. She had a childless marriage behind her; her ex-husband was a professor at the Sorbonne. It had been an amicable divorce, born out of weariness.

That night they had dinner. The next night they had dinner. And the third night they had dinner and went to bed. She was very good in bed – demanding much but receiving it rapturously. Their physical love bloomed, but they had a friendship too that grew in strength until Marius found it hard to travel. They understood each other in a mature way, thankful they had met now. Earlier or later would not have done. Now they were centred on each other and nothing very much on the outside mattered. They had known each other for almost a year now, and still Marius knew little of her husband, or her past life, and she knew little of his parents – or even much about the accusations that hovered in the suspicious air of St Esprit or the more political circles in Lyon. Neither of them had had a core to their lives, and now that they had one both were mutually fascinated by it. 'Something to come inside for,' she had once told him and Marius felt that Monique had expressed that core with perfection. Both men-tally and physically, what they had between them was defi-nitely 'something to come inside for'.

'I enjoyed our promenade.'

'So did I. I won't accompany you back.'

'No. There will be Mother to see to.'

'I shall visit her tomorrow.'

'That's good of you.' Marius took the old man's hand. It was dry and cool and strong. 'I know she'll have to go somewhere,' he added sadly.

'What about a live-in nurse?'

'Is that really practical? And it's bound to be hugely expensive. I've been thinking about getting them to sell for some time.'

'Are you still convinced that's right?' Alain sounded almost querulous.

'Father won't leave enough to restore the place. And you can't invite a nurse to live in a ruin.'

'It's not as bad as that.'

'It soon will be.'

'Marius . . .' They were walking across the field now, the old man limping slightly. 'Suppose we pooled resources?'

'What?'

'It's a shame to let her die in an institution.'

Marius was considerably startled. 'Yes, but what resources? I don't have any capital.'

'I have a lot,' said Alain quietly. 'Why don't you let me get the house back to what it was?'

'It would cost a fortune. And why should you?'

'For your mother. And when she dies, it will be a mutual investment and we can sell it on the open market.' He chuckled. 'We'll work out some kind of split. Of course Solange could outlive me. But then it will be an investment for Gaby. And yourself.'

Marius didn't know what to say. He reached out and took the old man's hand again.

'I would have done this while Henri was alive,' said Alain. 'But he wouldn't let me.'

'Why not?'

'Perhaps he thought it would incriminate me in some way. I told you – he was a good man. And you have to remember how strong our mutual chains of loyalty were, and how much he depended on my life-long support.'

'You are very generous.'

'Will you allow me?'

'Can I think it over?'

'Of course.'

They parted in the soft, fragrant moonlight and went back their separate ways. Marius turned to watch his dark receding shape. His limp was more pronounced now and suddenly he looked rather vulnerable.

Marius turned the idea over in his mind but all he could see was his father's face. The thought of the Château Letoric suddenly rising like a phoenix, clad in sandblasted masonry and overlooking pristine lawn and clear water, did not occur to him as a reality. Dissolution and decay seemed much more likely. A pang of guilt nudged Marius; what was he doing climbing hills with Alain when he should have been at home nursing his mother? Instead he had left the task to a slut. And not one with a heart of gold. His step quickened as Marius hurried towards the scarred overgrown pillars that marked the beginning of the stony track that had once been the gracious sweep of a drive up to Letoric. A shadow detached itself from the crumbling plaster. Jean-Pierre Claude.

6

'Marius?'

'What the hell do you want?'

'A talk.'

'This isn't the time.'

'You used to have a lot of time for me.'

'Yes.'

'A lot of time.' Jean-Pierre's voice was slurred.

Would there be a scene, wondered Marius. Suddenly he felt weary to the bone.

'Go home and sober up.'

'I wanted to let you know I was sorry. About your father.' There was an animal smell to him that Marius had always found alluring. If only he was drunk too, he thought wildly. When had he last gone to him? A year ago? And now the desire was there again. Slowly kindling. By the light of a cloud-strewn moon he could see Jean-Pierre was wearing a T-shirt and tight jeans, emphasising his gone-to-seed voluptuous figure. Marius looked down to his crotch. It was massive. He looked up and the sky seemed one swirling mass of night-flying vapour.

'Thank you.'

'I'm sorry about making demands on you. About the notes.'

'Look – '

'Don't you understand, I'm really sorry about that too.' There was something triumphant in his voice; he seemed like a truculent child making a false apology.

'I won't pay you.'

'We're very poor, Maman and I. You'll have to help us someday.'

'I shall go to the police.' And at that moment Marius suddenly realised he would. The decision made him feel powerful. Sexually powerful. Why in God's name hadn't he told Gabriel this morning? Why hadn't he gone to him before? Suddenly his mind was crystal clear and for the first time since the blackmail had started he was unafraid. His father was dead now – he couldn't be harmed. His mother was too far gone. And Monique? Monique would understand. The power in him swelled, and he smiled at Jean-Pierre who looked startled, despite his drunkenness. 'I shall go to the police tomorrow morning.'

'That would not be clever.'

'I should never have let this pass for so long. I only kept quiet to protect my father.' Marius knew he sounded absurdly pompous. I could have confided in Alain too, he thought. But a tremor filled him. Could he? Suppose Alain withdrew in disgust from the house offer? He would be plunging his mother into an institution.

Jean-Pierre looked at him blearily, unbelievingly. 'You wouldn't do it.'

'But I will. I have nothing to lose now.' The doubts consumed him but he was determined.

'It'll do you no good,' spluttered Jean-Pierre. His heavy, swarthy, unshaven face contorted with fleeting panic and growing lack of resolve. 'It'll damn you.'

'More likely you,' said Marius calmly. 'Blackmail is a criminal offence – in case you didn't know.'

'I'll break you.'

'Correction. I'll break you.' He advanced a few paces on him.

'You want me, don't you?' Jean-Pierre smiled a little wildly.

'Yes,' Marius said flatly. 'I want you on the grounds of sheer animal lust. That's all.'

'That's all? You've been at it for years – at me for years.'

'You're right. I haven't learnt to control it.' Suddenly Marius began to tremble. He was centimetres from Jean-Pierre now and he could smell the alcohol on his breath and the sweat on his body. Both he found exciting. Could he control himself? 'But I have to learn,' he said quietly.

'You've got a woman in Lyon.' He made the word 'woman' sound unutterably obscene.

'What if I've got one in Paris – and in Aix – and in Nice – as

74

well as Lyon?' Marius laughed humourlessly. 'What is it to you?'

'You won't keep your whores if they know you fuck men.'

Marius stared at Jean-Pierre for a minute without speaking, and suddenly the desire left him. Instead he felt deeply depressed. 'Go to hell,' he said at last, backing away. Catching his mood, Jean-Pierre tried a different tack.

'Come on – you can have me when you like. You know that. But you've got to pay.'

'Backdated?'

'If you put it like that. Maman and I – '

'Damn your mother.'

'Don't speak about her like that.'

Marius turned away but Jean-Pierre grabbed his shoulder and spun him round. As always, Marius was surprised by the man's strength, but this time he didn't find it erotic. An image of Monique's face swam into his mind. She was smiling her dry, funny smile.

'Leave me alone.' Marius pushed him away.

'I could kill you.' Jean-Pierre drunkenly lurched towards him.

'You couldn't kill a fly. Go home and sober up.'

'To hell with you.' He swung clumsily at Marius and missed.

'Go *home.*'

'You bastard.'

Marius knew that he had to walk away. Fast. He began to do so and he could hear Jean-Pierre shambling after him. Then he heard him fall and, still walking, turned round. Jean-Pierre had stumbled in one of the innumerable holes in the driveway and was lying on his back, cursing. He was a ludicrous, undignified sight.

'Help me,' he mumbled.

But Marius did not pause in his stride.

'I'll kill you,' he yelled. 'So help me God – I'll kill you.'

Marius walked faster.

'Mother?'

'Mm?'

'Has Estelle left you alone?'

'Who's Estelle? Is Henri in yet? He's been a long time walking in the forest. Is he with Alain? They always get talking – ' She dozed off again, her big frowsty figure humped under the sheets.

Marius passed his hand over her forehead. She was very hot and he wondered if she was running a temperature. 'Estelle?'

'Yes, monsieur?' She seemed to emerge out of the shadows of the room and he could smell cognac on her breath. She had probably been helping herself downstairs.

'Where have you been?'

'In Madame's bathroom – clearing up.' He could sense her pouting at him in the semi-darkness.

'Clearing up what?' he snapped.

'I gave her a bath.'

'She can manage herself, providing the door isn't locked.'

'Well, she couldn't tonight. And I doubt if she will again. Her system can't take the shock, you see.'

'I – ' Marius bit back the angry words. He would have to get a nurse in. But he might be dependent on Estelle for a few more days. He would have to handle her carefully. 'I'm grateful to you for staying on like this.'

'Do you want me to stay the night?'

'Er – '

'She could be up and down.'

Could he trust her, he wondered, reluctant to let her stay.

'I'm capable,' she said, reading his thoughts. On top of the drink he could smell her sweat. It made him think of Jean-Pierre. 'I could use the money – and you could use some sleep.' Her voice was gentler than before and he looked at her sharply. 'Can I get you something to eat?' she asked.

'I'm fine. I've been out walking. I'm tired.'

'Sure?'

'Yes, but thank you.' He paused looking down at his mother. 'How's she been?'

'Wandering. She may sleep now. For a bit.'

'Where will you – '

'I can make up the divan in here.'

'You sure?'

'I'm sure.'

'It's good of you – at this short notice.'

'You need a drink.' Her voice was soft.

76

Would there be anything left, he wondered ironically. 'I'll get a nightcap. And thanks again.'

He left the room quietly.

Strangely, Marius slept deeply. He awoke with a feeling of refreshed clarity and looked at his watch. It was just after seven-thirty. Marius knew what he had to do – ring Gabriel and Monique. In that order. He felt confident about his confession and as he opened the shutters and looked out over the ravaged garden, he wondered again about Alain's offer. To have all this restored to its original – well, not exactly glory but mellowness. Was it really a possibility? Just suppose he didn't sell, and brought in a nurse while Letoric was miraculously restored around him? He thought of Monique. Would they live here together one day? Dream or possibility, the conjecturing gave him an inner warmth – a bastion against the possibility of these two vital conversations going wrong.

Suddenly he could bear the delay no longer. He could ring Gabriel at home. Maybe that would be better anyway.

Isobelle Rodiet brought coffee to her husband's bedside. She had been up for hours, unable to sleep while he had tossed and turned throughout the night. Once he had half woken and she had heard him mutter his mother's name. Isobelle had thought of waking him, but then dismissed the idea. He had never talked about it, and this was perhaps not the right moment. She often thought she should broach the subject after they had lunched at Annette Valier's restaurant. They both looked for-ward to this regular Sunday treat – a treat that had become a tradition, only broken for a vacation or an illness. After the excellent meal they would often walk home, usually alone. That would be the time – but for many years she had been too frightened to raise the subject for she knew that it was some-thing he had banished. The restaurant was called Le Clozel. Originally a fortified farmhouse with a bell tower, it stood beside a sandy-beached river that in summer was little more than a trickling stream. Inside the tables were widely spaced in a cool, dark, high-ceilinged room. Outside they were crowded

77

on to a small stone terrace that looked across to the pine-clad rocky foothills of the Alps. Le Clozel was sun-bleached and its weathered stone was worn and smooth to the touch. Annette had bought the restaurant from Madame Mercier who had run it for forty years. She had made no changes, and the same chef – Madame Mercier's withered younger sister – presided over the kitchen at sixty and would no doubt do so for many years to come. She and Gabriel had been to Le Clozel under both regimes and would lunch with a group of friends which would sometimes include André Valier, if he was home, and more often Alain Leger. Henri had once been a regular at their table, but since the Lyon trial he had not appeared. The meals began at midday and would not end till four. In the winter they would sit longer but in the spring, summer and autumn, they would stroll along the river's sandy shores, taking a bottle of Calvados down to the stone tables and benches that were scattered along the beach – the third level of Le Clozel. They would talk, up to a dozen of them, sometimes more. Later, wearied by conversation, by ideas, by standpoints, they would silently watch the clear stream flow in its gutted bed. But last Sunday he had not gone, pleading paperwork – a previously unheard-of occupation at lunchtime on a Sunday. The thought of missing one of the Mercier lunches would once have been a sacrilege to him.

Gabriel finally rolled over and opened his eyes. Gratefully he sat up and sipped at his coffee.

Isobelle loved him distractedly. She always had. He had been a wonderful father, was – could still be – a wonderful lover. He was also a good companion. Often surrounded by other people, she had longed to be with him on her own. Yet there had always been this barrier about his mother.

'I don't want to talk about it,' he had told her in the very early years of their marriage. 'Ever.' And he never had. Yet there was something happening now. Clearly the Larche affair had brought the past back into the present. He was suffering – and she felt completely shut out.

'What's the matter?' she asked.

'Work.'

'Nothing to do with Henri Larche?'

'I'm sad. He was a good man. It proves there are darker feelings here than I thought.'

'Perhaps it was an outsider.'

'I doubt it.'

'And Marius? How has he taken it all?' Strangely, they had hardly discussed what had happened. Gabriel had been back too late the night before and, in the end, she had not sat up waiting for him. She had left bread and pâté and cheese and red wine, but not much of it had been touched.

'He's very shaken.'

Isobelle barely knew Marius Larche. For most of his home visits he had kept to the house; the rest of the time he travelled or lived in Lyon. She knew him as a high-ranking policeman – but in a completely different sphere to Gabriel.

'Lebatre's in charge,' he said, drinking more coffee and yawning. 'He's a sound man.'

The telephone rang by the bedside and Gabriel checked her move to pick it up.

'Let me have it,' he said wearily. 'It'll probably be Lebatre.'

'Gabriel?'

'Yes?'

'I'm sorry to ring you at home. It's Marius Larche.'

'That's all right. Have there been any – developments?'

'I have something to tell you.'

'Oh?'

Marius paused. In a few seconds it would be over, whatever the consequences. His new-found confidence had largely deserted him. 'I should have told you this before.'

'Do you want me to come over?'

'I'd rather talk about it on the phone.'

'You appreciate I put Lebatre in charge of the case?' His voice held gentle, reluctant admonishment.

'Yes. But I need to talk to you. I'm sorry.'

'Don't be sorry. I'm listening.'

'I've been – someone is blackmailing me.'

'I see.' There was no expression in Gabriel's voice, instead a comforting neutrality.

'It's been going on since I got back – say, a couple of weeks.' Marius was speaking more crisply now, as if he was giving professional evidence. 'There were three notes, demanding money with menaces. I didn't pay anything.'

'Do you know who was making the demands?'

'Jean-Pierre Claude.'

'Ah.' For once, Gabriel seemed hesitant. 'Wouldn't it be better if we talked this over face to face?'

'I'd rather give you the details now. They're not very – pleasant. We could talk – later. When I've . . .' His voice tailed away.

'Go on.' Gabriel sounded inviting and more positive. 'What was the content of the notes?'

'Asking for money. A considerable sum. The notes were left in the conservatory.'

'Where your father was murdered?'

'Yes.'

'Did you keep the notes?'

'Yes.'

'It would have been better if you had told me this yesterday.'

'I realise that.' Marius's voice was sharp.

'What did he know?'

'He knew that – over a period of years, I had – had – relations with him. I had homosexual relations with him.'

'I see.' Gabriel sounded very matter of fact and for a moment Marius was reassured. Then his reassurance was shattered. 'You do realise this could have a bearing on your father's death?'

'Yes.'

'These notes – they were spaced out over a period of – two weeks?'

'Yes. Two last week. Tuesday and Thursday. And the other, the day before yesterday.

'Have you seen Claude since the notes arrived?'

'Last night. For the first time. He accosted me. I'd been for a walk with Alain Leger. On the way back, he was waiting for me, very drunk. I told him I wasn't paying – and was going to the police.'

'Pity you didn't do that much earlier – you've been very foolish, Marius.'

'I was bloody terrified.' Marius felt the blood pounding in his temples. 'And I hoped he'd go away.'

80

'Unlikely.' The mocking note was gone.

'I realise that . . .' Marius' voice faltered for the first time.

'You're prepared to go through the courts?'

'If I have to.'

'Do *you* think Claude had anything to do with your father's murder?'

'My father hardly knows Claude – and he would never be raised from his bed by him, and follow him outside. The idea is ludicrous.'

'But not impossible. I'll get Lebatre to see Claude today.'

'Very well. And again – I'm sorry not to have brought this up earlier.'

'It's not easy for you. Do you want to see me again today?'

'I think the question is – do you want to see me?'

'I've no doubt Lebatre will. By the way, Marius, are you staying at the house for the next few days?'

'What do you think? But wasn't it you and Lebatre who would have preferred me in Lyon?'

'Things change,' said Gabriel as he prepared to wind up the conversation.

When he had put the phone down, Isobelle said: 'What was all that?'

'Marius Larche. Confessing to blackmail. He's been having a homosexual affair with some yokel. Does that surprise you?'

'Not particularly.'

'Why not?' His remoteness had temporarily disappeared and he seemed anxious to hear what she had to say.

'He's that kind of man. You can't feel his sensuality. Women know,' she said abruptly.

'So you could have told me he was gay.'

'Not gay necessarily. Perhaps he's bisexual. Doesn't he have someone in Lyon? A girl-friend?'

Gabriel got out of bed and put on a dressing gown. 'This case . . .' he began.

'Well?'

'It frightens me.'

'It's very close to home,' she replied. 'For all of us,' she added. He was silent and she didn't press him. She would await her opportunity.

*

81

'Monique.' Marius was sweating, despite the fact that it was still early. Somewhere he could hear his mother shuffling around and Estelle banging downstairs. He was deeply conscious of the fact that he should have called her before – that he should not have allowed her to read it in the press. But he hadn't wanted to call – hadn't wanted to set a chain of events rolling that perhaps he couldn't control – to admit that Letoric and the blackmail notes and now the butchering of his father had spun a cocoon around him.

'Marius, I've been trying to call you. I had to go out of town and didn't see the press until late last night and – ' Her stumbling explanation seemed to go on forever.

'It's all right. I should have called you yesterday – it's just been so terrible. Such a terrible shock.'

'God. Why?' Despite her agitation, her voice was rich and controlled. He had always found her voice quite wonderful. 'I must have tried to phone a dozen times last night but the phone seemed permanently engaged. Then I overslept this – '

'That was probably Estelle, informing all and sundry.'

'I'm so terribly sorry. To think it happened – after all.'

'After all?'

'I just thought – all those rumours and press speculation. That would be the end of it. I want to come out. This morning.'

'I'd rather you didn't.'

'But why?' She sounded very hurt.

'I want to tell you something.'

'Yes?'

'I've been blackmailed – by a local peasant.'

'A girl?' She laughed uneasily.

'A man.'

'Yes?' The trepidation in her voice deepened now, or was he imagining it?

'I've had – some encounters with him.'

'I don't understand.'

'Sex.'

'Oh.'

'It's over. It should never have started.'

'Why did it?' Her voice was gentle and he felt encouraged.

'I don't know. He's the only man I've ever been with. It

hasn't happened for a long time. But before that – sporadically. Since I was a boy.'

'Do you ever see him – feel him – when *we* are making love?'

'No,' he said eventually, vehemently. 'Not ever. I promise you.'

'You didn't have to promise me. I believed you. I know you, Marius.'

'You couldn't know that,' he said bluntly.

'I'm not sure – obviously I didn't know anything about this, but there *was* a reservation.'

'When we made love?'

'Just a reservation,' she repeated.

'God – '

'Perhaps there won't be now.' She was wistful.

'There *won't* be.'

'Marius . . .'

'Yes?'

'It's not a dirty secret.'

'I think it is.'

'But it's not.'

'*So* – we live in an enlightened age?' There was a hint of irony in his voice.

'It's nothing to do with that,' she said emphatically. 'Don't you understand?'

'Yes. I think I do.'

'I *must* see you.'

'No.'

'But why?' She sounded deeply hurt.

'The police will be here a lot. They're furious with me.'

'But you know him. Rodiet, isn't it?'

'It doesn't make any difference. I should have told them.'

'Does it connect?'

'They think it might.'

'That *he* killed your father? But why – if he wanted to squeeze money out of you?'

'That's *my* point. But Rodiet thinks he could have killed him as some kind of warning – because I hadn't paid up.'

'Rubbish. I've never heard such a cock-eyed theory in my life.' She paused and then said more tentatively, 'Marius . . .'

'Yes?'

83

'*Did* you pay him anything?'

'No.'

'Will they arrest him?'

'For blackmail. Maybe. But for murder – God knows.'

'I *must* come. You can't exclude me from this.'

But Marius was adamant. 'I'll come to you in Lyon. Soon. I don't want you mixed up in this sordid mess.'

She continued to argue but he was ruthless; he had to be. Monique was the future, she was also another world. He didn't want her colliding with this one. Perhaps when it was all over – if it was ever all over – and if he took up Alain's offer, then her arrival was a possibility. But until then Marius wanted to see it through alone.

Marius wandered down into the overgrown garden. It was a particularly clear day and he could see the Alps. There was a pristine clarity to everything and he noticed that the unpruned, weed-choked flower-beds had managed to produce some perfect blooms. A lizard lay poised on one of the crumbling walls of the Château Letoric and the hard sunlight made the broken statues, the undergrowth-shrouded cherubs look benignly ancient. Sitting on the moss-and-lichen-covered steps, Marius watched ants scurry, somehow officiously, up and over the dislodged stonework. Then he reluctantly rose to his feet and went indoors to see what mood and what mental state his mother was in this morning.

He heard voices inside the little sitting-room and paused. Then Marius opened the door to find Alain and his mother drinking coffee round the circular antique polished table that his father had treasured so much. He remembered as a child being allowed to sit round it and then spilling blackcurrant cordial on its lustrous surface. His father had been furious, but Marius was undismayed. He partly resented this unexpected burst of anger from a man who was generally so distant but he was also pleased to have produced a spark of feeling in him at least.

Now Alain was half standing up and his mother was leaning forward, staring at him very intently. Marius was surprised to see such a sudden change in her.

84

'I'm sorry,' said Alain, limping towards Marius as he opened the door. He looked tired and his usually good physique for once seemed slouched. 'Estelle let me in. Do you remember – '

'Of course,' replied Marius quickly. 'I knew you were coming to see Mother. It's I who should apologise for not being here to receive you.'

'He's been dining with us,' said Solange, and Marius' heart sank. She seemed very excited and kept pushing her frowsy hair out of her eyes. 'Is Henri in the lavatory?' she asked.

'I must go.' Alain limped painfully back to Solange. He bent over and kissed her. 'God bless you,' he said.

Marius heard a slight noise from behind the hatch. Clearly Estelle had been listening attentively as usual.

'Madame Claude?'

'Well?'

'I am Inspector Lebatre.'

'What do you want?'

'To see your son.'

'He's not well. He's in bed.'

'What's the matter with him?' said Lebatre sharply.

'Flu.' She stood on the steps of the low-raftered building, her arms folded over her apron, clearly prepared to defy him.

'I'm sorry. But I have to see him.'

Her small dark eyes studied him, and then she stepped back, allowing Lebatre to plunge into the stale gloom.

'Thank you.'

'You mustn't stay long.'

'I won't.'

She showed him into a small, stuffy room on the ground floor. The alcohol fumes hit Lebatre as he walked in. Jean-Pierre was lying in a sozzled heap, a dirty blanket half slung over him.

'Monsieur Claude?'

He turned over, bleary and bloodshot of eye. 'Who the hell are you?'

'Inspector Lebatre of the Aix Securité. I want to talk to you. Now.'

*

He sat on the edge of the bed, wrapped in an eiderdown that had been lying on the floor.

'I'm not myself,' he said.

'No.'

The old lady stood by the door, immovable as a block of granite. Lebatre turned to her. 'Will you leave us?'

'He's my son. What do you want with him?'

'I asked you to leave us.'

Silently, and with many a backward glance, she shuffled away. It was only when Lebatre had reassured himself that she was safely out of earshot that he resumed his inquisition of the bleary-eyed Jean-Pierre.

'I want to talk to you about Marius Larche.'

'What about him?'

'He's the man you tried to blackmail.'

Jean-Pierre laughed in a gulping sort of way and his hand went to his eyes in an odd gesture, as if he was trying to brush something away.

'I hardly know him.'

'Larche has spoken to us.'

'What about?' The puzzled expression was crudely simulated.

'You know what about.' Lebatre didn't feel patient. He was already in a bad mood. What was he supposed to be? Some kind of lackey? Larche had confided in Rodiet – and Rodiet had given him instructions to interview Claude. It was clearly going to be that kind of case. And now he was cooped up with this drunken peasant, who exuded both halitosis and body odour.

'I've never blackmailed – '

Lebatre got up briskly and closed the door. He then walked back to the bed, grabbed Jean-Pierre round the throat and shook him. His eyes started out of his head until Lebatre released his grip and he came up spluttering.

'You assaulted me.'

'I've hardly started.'

'I shall make a complaint to your superiors – '

'Do that.'

'You can't treat – '

'I shall do it again. But next time my fingers will jam around your windpipe. It won't be pleasant. Do we understand each other?'

Jean-Pierre started to protest and then changed his mind. He nodded unhappily instead.

'When did you start blackmailing him?'

'A couple of weeks ago.'

'Why?'

'He's mistreated me.'

'How?'

'I – gave him what he wanted. I've been doing it for years. Did he tell you that?'

'Yes.'

Jean-Pierre looked disconcerted. Then he stumbled on. 'He left us in the lurch.'

'What do you mean by that?' Lebatre's tone was contemptuous.

'We're poor people – '

'You wanted payment for sex.'

'It would have – it was only right.'

'So you sent him threatening notes.'

'I've waited for years.'

'Does your mother know about this?'

'Of course.'

'I'm surprised.' Lebatre was genuinely amazed. Mothers were sacred to him. They didn't – shouldn't – know about things like this. He looked angrily at Jean-Pierre. 'Larche has told us everything.'

'I'm sure I can tell you more.'

'Perhaps you can. Where were you early yesterday morning?'

Jean-Pierre stared at him with dawning horror in his eyes.

'You suspect me – of killing the old man?' His voice was shrill.

'Perhaps,' said Lebatre nonchalantly.

'But why should I? I would have everything to lose by his death.' He sounded melodramatic now.

'Would you?' returned Lebatre coolly. 'Marius Larche wasn't paying, so maybe you killed the old man in revenge.'

'Nonsense. Larche would have paid in the end.'

'I doubt it. Get dressed.'

'Where are you taking me?'

'To the Gendarmerie. I want you to sign a statement.'

'I didn't touch the old man.'

'You wrote blackmail notes. That's a criminal offence.'

'I didn't kill him – '

'We can discuss that. Get some clothes on.'

'What about Maman?'

'To hell with your mother.' Lebatre advanced on him threateningly and Jean-Pierre hurriedly clambered out of bed.

Lebatre phoned Marius a couple of hours later from the Gendarmerie. The afternoon was intensely hot and Marius had been dozing on the terrace at the back of the house. Around his feet, nature had almost entirely taken back the terrace and through the cracks in the concrete protruded a variety of tiny, vigorous wild flowers.

When the telephone began to ring Marius hesitated. Why not let it ring? The old lady was sound asleep and it wouldn't disturb her. Estelle had gone shopping. Then, reluctantly, he rose to his feet and went inside.

'It's Lebatre.'

'Ah.'

'I have Claude down here.'

'Are you holding him?'

'Well, he's committed a criminal offence.' Lebatre's voice was challenging. 'He's made a statement, and if you'll do the same I'll charge him.'

'What will he get?'

'Sentence? Up to five years. Maybe more.'

Marius considered. 'Is all this unavoidable?'

There was a harder edge to Lebatre's voice as he replied. 'You contacted us – I've questioned the wretched man – and he's admitted the offence. If you back out now, you'll be wasting police time. And you of all people should realise the importance of police time.'

'Yes. But I'm also thinking of his mother. How could she support herself if he went into jail?'

'The State will support her.'

'I'm sorry,' he told Lebatre. 'I should know better. I'll come down and make a statement.'

'Then we'll charge him.' Lebatre was friendlier. 'I would like to get this over with. I have a major investigation on my hands. As you know.'

'Yes. I understand. I'll come down right away.'

'There is one thing – '

'Well?'

'There may be a bail application. From his mother. She would have to make it on the strength of her property. I believe they own the house.'

'I believe they do.'

'I have to remind you – I don't need to remind you – that you mustn't – '

'See him? For what purpose?' Suddenly he wanted to make Lebatre's life harder than it already was.

'Er – he's only at the end of the road. He may approach you – ask for your help.'

'I'll be wary.'

'I have to cover all the ground.'

'Of course you do. I'll be with you in half an hour.'

Marius put down the phone. His hands were shaking and there was sweat running down his forehead. It had nothing to do with the heat.

'Estelle.' Silence.

'Estelle.'

The kitchen was in a dreadful state. The washing up had not been done for what looked like days and there was congealed food on the plates on the table. Flies buzzed over the debris. What the hell was he going to do? Clear it up himself? Force her to do it? Find someone else? But who? He looked at his watch. Almost four.

'Estelle!'

But there was still no sign of her. Really, it was too bad. First thing tomorrow he would start organising. Get a nurse for his mother. A new domestic. And he would sack Estelle with the greatest of pleasure. Tomorrow. Wrenching his eyes away from the mess, Marius walked out of the house and down the drive. In his mind's eye, the irritating image of Estelle was replaced by Monique. Yes, he would have given anything to have her with him now. But no – he must resist the temptation. She mustn't be mixed up with the past. The past that was still his present.

*

'They've taken him.' Mariola was beside herself, wringing her hands at her battered front door while Estelle, still mounted on her bicycle, listened aghast. When the old woman had finished the story, she got off, leant the bicycle against the wall and held Mariola in her arms. It would wait, what she had to tell her. But it wouldn't wait long.

7

Gabriel was there to meet him in the Gendarmerie at Aix. Marius was surprised, having expected the taciturn Lebatre. He took Marius into a comfortable room, with sofas and chairs and reproductions of Impressionist paintings on the walls.

'I haven't been in here before.'

'It's my conference room.'

'Do people usually make statements in here?'

'No. But you will.'

'Why?'

'I want you to be comfortable.'

'Is that why Lebatre isn't here?' asked Marius, amused.

'He has a lot of work on. The investigation into your father's murder for instance.'

'And so you are taking my statement.'

'I thought it would be easier for everybody.'

'Thank you.' Marius sat down on the sofa, suddenly feeling exhausted. 'Where is Claude?'

'You won't have to see him.'

'That's good. But is he going to get bail?'

'Probably. He won't come to court for months. He won't bother you.' Gabriel sat down at a small desk in the corner of the room and fidgeted with a paperweight. 'I admire you, Marius,' he said.

'For what?'

'Owning up. Not letting yourself be brow-beaten by that slob of a peasant.'

'He's never had a chance.'

'He's never given himself one. Make your statement and don't give him another thought.'

'I shall have to come to court.'

'Not if I have anything to do with it,' said Gabriel firmly.

'You mean you can keep me out of it?'

'I can try. I'm sorry about it all.'

'I'm sorry for Claude. I used him.'

'He had no right to blackmail you.'

'It was predictable. They haven't got any money.'

'Lebatre said you were concerned about the old woman. But don't worry. She'll be looked after. You have to remember that – '

'Shall we get on with the statement,' interrupted Marius abruptly.

'Of course. But I thought you would – like a drink first.'

Need, thought Marius hopelessly. *Need* a drink first – that's what he means. But of course I do need one. He smiled. 'I'd like that.'

'I'll join you.' Gabriel rose and went to a cupboard. 'I have some pastis – I thought that would be right for both of us.'

'Aren't you rather going over Lebatre's head?' asked Marius.

'Absolutely,' replied Gabriel, pouring the drinks.

'Mariola?'

'Madame Claude to you.'

She was in the small kitchen garden that was at the rear of the cottage. Lebatre looked round appreciatively, inhaling the rich, aromatic smell. 'You've got quite a herb garden here.'

'Where is my son?'

'At Aix – in the Gendarmerie. As you know.'

'When will he be home?'

'When bail is arranged. They will need your title deeds as I told you on the phone.'

'They are inside.'

It was just after five and the heat was intense. But the sharp, hazy, bitter-sweet smell of the herbs detained him. Lebatre was a man who liked his food and his wife was an excellent cook, but he was wondering what culinary skills old Madame Claude had. He imagined she would be good with poultry, with hare or rabbit, adding the musky essence of the herbs to roasted animal flesh.

'Quite a herb garden here.'

'It belongs to Jean-Pierre. He tends it with love . . .' Her voice shook. 'He was wrong to write those notes. What will he get?'

'Perhaps not long. After all, no money changed hands. I gather you knew what was going on.'

'Yes.'

'And you approved?'

'It was between my son and Marius Larche.'

'That's no answer. Do you realise how lucky you are I'm not arresting you too?'

She turned away from him, shrugging. Then she whispered: 'Will they let him off?'

'Demanding money with menaces? I don't think so. And the notes were left in the conservatory, where the old man met his death.'

'You don't suspect him of that?' Her voice was shrill.

'I would hope to eliminate him from our enquiries – with your help.'

'What can I do?' She sat down on an old kitchen chair in the scented garden, folding her hands on her lap like a humbled child. Lebatre sat gingerly on the edge of an upturned rain barrel. A bee buzzed contentedly, drunk on pollen.

'His movements – early morning – yesterday.'

'He was here – all night – with me. He didn't get up for work till late – almost half-past seven.'

'Any other witnesses?'

She shook her head, her eyes fixed on him, knowing that her answer was not good enough. 'I swear to you he never left his bed.'

'How can you be sure of that?'

'Because I don't sleep. Not well. I wake at five – and usually go down to make myself coffee.'

'But why should you go to his room?'

She paused a little uneasily. 'I've got used to checking him.'

'Why?'

'Because he would go into Aix and not come back till all hours. I was always worried about him.'

'Why?' asked Lebatre bleakly.

'I never knew what he was doing.' She was staring down at

the baked earth. A slight breeze wafted the smell of lavender to him from the field behind the house.

'Are you telling me the truth?'

'The truth?' she hedged.

'Yes. Surely you knew what he was doing?'

'Drinking,' she grunted.

'And?' prompted Lebatre.

'Whoring.'

'But with what sex?'

'Women, of course – '

'Come on, Mariola – '

'Don't *call* me that.'

'You *know* what he was doing. If you're trying to help him, don't lie to me. He was a male prostitute, wasn't he?'

She said nothing, still staring down at the earth.

'Please . . .'

Then she looked up. And her eyes were screwed up with pain.

'Do I *have* to say that?'

'It's the truth, isn't it?' said Lebatre patiently. Yet he felt for her. His own mother was alive in a small village not too far from Aix. Supposing his path had been Jean-Pierre's?

She nodded and then spoke bitterly. 'It's his father who was to blame.'

'Why?'

'He did things to him. When he was a child.'

'You mean he interfered with him?'

She nodded again. 'He was a brute of a man.'

'Where is he now?'

'He left us. Went to work as a builder. Now he's dead.'

'Jean-Pierre. Does he work?'

'Yes, he has a job on a farm. He drives a tractor.'

'Is the job good?'

'It's hard work.'

'He's always kept it?'

'Monsier Roche – he is tolerant.'

'That means there have been times – '

'My son drinks. Too much.' She sighed. 'Now he'll lose the job.'

94

'You'll be all right. You've got a pension, haven't you? If he goes inside there'll be something.'

She shrugged. 'So I'll be all right?' She looked at him blankly. 'What shall I do without my son?'

Lebatre looked away. 'When did all this business with Marius Larche begin?'

'Years ago.'

'Did money change hands?'

'No. That's why he felt owed.'

'Would you describe your son as bisexual?'

'That he has been with women as well? I think he has. He says he has.' She paused. 'I hope he has.'

'Why did he begin to try and blackmail Larche?'

'Jean-Pierre felt he had been used – used too much by a man who should have been paying for his pleasure. We are very poor. Getting poorer.'

'And so – didn't he want rather a lot?'

'It was absurd. I told him it was absurd.' Lebatre noticed she was trying to disclaim responsibility now. 'But he probably wrote the notes when he was drunk. And let's face it, my son was drunk an awful lot of the time.'

'You'd testify to that?'

'If it would help. Would it?' She seized the straw.

'It might. Do you think he would agree to be hospitalised?'

'A dry-out?' She laughed.

'Rather than going to prison?' insisted Lebatre.

'Are you serious?'

'Yes.'

'You're a good man.' Suddenly she was animated. 'What about Larche?'

'He's already said he wants to drop charges.'

She stared at him, shocked. The sudden hope she radiated made him feel ill. 'Will he?'

'He can't.'

'Why not?' she beseeched.

'Because Larche reported him and he confessed. But if we could say your son was an alcoholic. I mean – you can count on Larche's sympathy.'

'Sympathy!' she flashed out. 'That rich bastard – and him a policeman too.'

'Do you *want* your son to go to prison?'

'You know I don't.'

'Then you have to co-operate.'

'With my son a suspect for murder. On top of everything else?' She looked at him hopelessly.

'I want to eliminate him as a suspect,' Lebatre snapped. 'Come on – pull yourself together, Mariola.'

This time she did not object to the use of her first name and he realised, with some regret, that he had broken her pride. Now she was staring at him abjectly.

'What can I tell you?' she asked.

'I want to know if he hated Larche.'

'Yes – he had grown to. Over the years. As his health broke down.'

'As his drinking increased?'

'That's what I mean.'

'Did he ever threaten his family?'

'No. His hate was directed at Marius Larche. I happen to know he felt sorry for the old man.'

'Sorry?' asked Lebatre incredulously.

'Yes. He was sorry for him.'

'I find that hard to believe.'

'So you may. But it's true. I was also surprised. As the rumours grew about Henri Larche, I was very quick to condemn him. I knew your boss's mother, for instance. Suzanne. She was a domineering woman but she had courage. She interfered in something very dangerous – and lost her life.'

'Do you believe Henri Larche presided over that tribunal?'

She paused and then said slowly, 'Yes, I do.'

'Do you have evidence?'

'None. But he seemed very thick with the Boche to me. And him with a wife in the Resistance.'

'Were you in it?'

'As much as I could be. My husband was. He may have been a bastard pig of a man, but he was brave in those times. He and Solange Larche and the others – they blew up the railway line. Not once but twice.'

'Why *should* Henri Larche have been – as you put it – thick with the Boche?'

'He was a great friend of the Commandant in Aix – Kummel.

They used to lunch together – he was the man they tried in Lyon.'

'How do you know all this?'

'Because I was a waitress at Le Clozel during the war. It had been commandeered as a headquarters for the Nazis.'

'Have you told anyone this before?'

'I thought it was common knowledge. I certainly talked it over with Jean-Pierre.'

'And?'

'Oh, he thought it was innocent enough.'

'How *could* it have been?'

'Just a friendship, he said.'

'A very dangerous one.'

'Jean-Pierre thought it was deliberate, so that he could find out information – and pass it on to Solange.'

'And what do you think?'

'I listened as much as I could – and I never heard anything being discussed. But I *did* hear them discussing the shootings.'

'And?'

'Henri said those responsible should be tried. Quickly.'

'Unofficially?'

'I didn't hear that.'

'And yet your son was sorry for him?'

'He felt it unfair to pick on an old man. He said something else.'

'Well?'

'He said there was someone else responsible for the – for the – executions.'

'Someone else? Someone who presided over the court?'

'I don't know – he didn't make it clear.'

'Do you mind if I use your phone?' he got up quickly.

She shrugged. 'Go ahead. Will you be wanting me again?'

'Yes,' he said. 'Directly I've finished this call.'

As he went out, Mariola was very conscious of not mentioning Didier. But there would be too many repercussions if she did.

Gabriel put down the phone.

'That was Lebatre,' he said.

Marius looked up from his statement. 'Well?'

'Madame Claude – she's come up with something.'

Marius looked apprehensive. 'Yes?'

'Apparently your father used to lunch with Kummel. Wolfgang Kummel – during the occupation – at Le Clozel. Did you know that?'

'No. I had no idea he even knew him – he was never asked to give evidence at the Lyon trial.' Marius stared at Gabriel, the raw onset of fear and astonishment trickling through his stomach. 'That old bitch,' he said, his voice shaking. 'What the hell does she know?'

'You're quite sure you never knew, Marius?'

'Of course I'm sure.' Marius felt sick and there was a crushing weight in his heart and in his head.

'Would your mother remember these meetings?' asked Gabriel.

'Unlikely.'

'Anyone else?'

'Alain Leger might know.'

'Will you ask him?'

'Yes, but – how significant is this?' asked Marius uneasily.

'Very,' said Gabriel drily. 'So significant that I think, on second thoughts, I should ask him myself.'

'You really believe my father collaborated, don't you? And if he did you've got cause to hate him – ' Marius spoke bitterly but he was bone-weary now and his emotions seemed one-dimensional.

'I don't think I have. My mother went to her death as she had lived – a bully. As I told you, I had very little affection for her.' He sipped his pastis ruminatively. 'Of course she was very brave. A heroine, like your own mother.' He paused, sunk deep in reflection, and Marius waited patiently until he returned to the present. 'Did your mother often talk about her experiences?' he asked finally.

'Never.'

'I wonder why?'

'You should know why. The question mark about my father must have been in her mind well before the rumours began – ever since the end of the war.'

Gabriel nodded. 'Whoever killed him may have been waiting

in the wings since the war. We've been doing some research on the families of those six young men who were shot – and we're coming up with some information about them. I'm leaving Lebatre to concentrate locally now and I'm putting an enquiry team on those families, however scattered they are. We shall have to account for all their movements. It's going to take a while.'

'I feel so powerless.' Marius looked down at the statement he had made on Jean-Pierre.

'Yes,' said Gabriel slowly. 'I'm sorry I can't allow you off the leash.' He paused. 'Marius – there is one thing you can do for me.'

'Well?'

'Does your mother have *any* periods of clarity?'

'Very few.'

'Talk to her about your father. Ask her what she *really* feels.'

'I don't think I'll come up with anything useful.'

'Try. And talk to Alain.'

'So you *are* letting me off the leash.' Marius smiled. It was now an unfamiliar facial movement and he felt stiff and self-conscious.

'In a very limited way,' replied Gabriel. He did not return the smile.

Mariola Claude telephoned Marie Leger towards the end of the afternoon. They were both members of a small women's club in St Esprit that met regularly for talk and craft activity in the back of the Café de Paix. But however engrossing the demonstrations of sewing or silk making or weaving or flower arranging were, it was the talk that they all fed on. The St Esprit Women's Circle was particularly vociferous and Mariola and Marie had gravitated towards each other very quickly. Both bored, both bitter, they pooled their rancour and each emerged more stoical as a result. Now seeking further comfort, Mariola filled in every detail of her son's arrest, the possible solution to an impending sentence and his drink problem, the involvement of Marius Larche and her own impossible position.

When she eventually paused for much-need breathing space Marie broke in with enthusiastic commiseration and astute questions about the nature of the charges. It was only towards the end of the long call that Mariola introduced the subject of Didier.

'Estelle tells me Solange told Henri that "Didier knows it wasn't you."'

'Now that I *don't* understand,' said Marie excitedly. 'He's always said it was.'

'I haven't told the police.'

'Are you going to?'

'No, but I'll tell you something in confidence.'

'What's that?' Marie's voice hissed out in a new surge of rabid curiosity.

'My Jean-Pierre. He's been to see him.'

'Why?'

'To try and find out what he *really* knows.'

'With what end in view?'

Mariola was silent. Then she began to explain.

'This is a funeral feast.'

'For Henri?' André Valier frowned at his wife over the white paper tablecloth. It was nine and the Valiers were dining with the Leger sisters at Le Clozel. The evening was humid and thunder clouds hung over the crowded terrace. The dinner had been organised by André. He had been very excited when he had phoned Annette earlier.

'I've had an idea.'

'What?' she had asked bleakly.

'I'm going to run a piece on Henri Larche tomorrow – something retrospective.' He had stroked the goatee beard in the way he often did when he was worried.

'You mean speculative?'

'I'll write it myself.' He had ignored her derision; she doubted if he had even noticed it. 'But I need to talk to the Leger sisters.'

'I think that could be a mistake. They're both very emotional.'

'Perhaps. Will you invite them to Le Clozel tonight?'

'They wouldn't come. They hardly know us.'

'Don't they sell cushions in that shop of theirs?'

'They may well do.' Annette's voice had been resigned. She

knew what was coming. The question was – would she accept it? And if she didn't, maybe he would withdraw altogether.

'I'll buy the restaurant some. Or the paper will.' He laughed without any obvious sign of humour.

'It may be too last-minute an idea for them.'

'I'm sure you can convince the ladies that – a certain flexibility would be to their advantage.'

And of course she had convinced them. Very easily – particularly when the Leger sisters discovered how many cushions she was thinking of buying. Now as they made somewhat stilted conversation, lubricated by André's studied charm, over a very good *daube*, Annette sat back and watched him skilfully bring the action to a head, realising at the same time how much they had grown apart for she had not seen him in action for a long time. He alternately teased and flattered the sisters until dumpy Marie was a gauche mass of blushing confusion and even the more sophisticated Mireille was coyly amused.

Slightly sickened, Annette looked down to the lower terrace on the river-bank with its cluttered fairy lights and huddled wooden tables. Twilight was deepening. The river was slow flowing and silent. Occasionally a fish jumped and broke the calm and sometimes muted conversation rose to a muffled shriek of laughter. But little else intruded on her thoughts as she watched a moth fly high over their table which was a little apart from the others – as instructed by André. She forced her attention back to the conversation – she instinctively realised it was potential good copy.

'And so – someone finally caught up with Henri Larche.' He paused for simulated reflection, while Mireille Leger looked away – and her sister sparkled with anticipation.

'Not before time,' she said, delighted to have the opportunity to discuss her favourite subject.

'Marie – ' her sister remonstrated, but there was no spirit in her voice. Clearly, thought Annette, she is only going through the motions of disapproving of her sister's indiscretion. And this is only the beginning, she thought dully.

'Of course, you knew him.'

'I knew him all right. He helped my brother swindle us out of our share of the estate. Now we're a couple of paupers.'

'Oh Marie – it's not as bad as all that,' sighed her sister. For a moment Mireille caught Annette's eye. Then she looked away. Had there been an appeal there, Annette wondered. But there was obviously no stopping Marie now. She's playing straight into André's hands, she thought.

'Yes,' said André confidingly. 'I heard some rumours about that too.'

'Of course I wrote Henri Larche some letters I should never have written.'

'Marie – '

'Well, it's public knowledge, isn't it? I see no point in denying anything. I'm impetuous.' She smiled unrepentantly, drawing her squat frame in, fingering her neck, eyes lowered.

Annette shivered. Why did André always prey on the weak?

'I can quite understand how angry you must have been.' André's voice was quietly neutral. 'You've been deprived of your rights.'

'Henri Larche got his just desserts.' Marie picked at the food. 'It's not murder. It's justice.'

'Marie – ' Again her sister protested but André cut across her quickly.

'I'm thinking of running a piece on Larche. I wonder if you would care to come into the office tomorrow and talk about him – for an editorial fee, of course.'

There was a long silence during which Annette had the wild hope Marie might turn him down. She also wondered if Mireille was thinking the same thing.

'But I don't know anything about what happened in the war.' She spoke gruffly, defensively. 'Beyond what other people have said, of course.'

'I was thinking of another angle.'

'The estate?'

'You couldn't possibly,' said Mireille. 'Alain would be involved.'

'To hell with him.' Marie took another defiant sip of wine. To hell with my digestion too, she thought triumphantly.

'There would be legal trouble – '

André turned his charm on Mireille. He's approaching her differently, thought Annette, with a kind of awful boyish honesty. She shivered again. 'Of course we'd have our lawyer check it out.'

102

'Monsieur Valier,' began Mireille, 'what is the purpose of this – interview with my sister?'

'You're very welcome to come along yourself,' he hastened to assure her. 'We'd be glad to – '

'No. I don't want to get involved. And you haven't answered my question.' She sounded quite sharp and Annette smiled, hastily wiping it from her face before André saw. But she needn't have bothered, she told herself. He hadn't looked at her all the evening.

'I'm going to run a series called "Henri Larche – Judge on the Edge" – or something like that.' André paused. 'This might be your sister's view, one of his victims – '

'Hang on,' said Annette suddenly, determined not to finish the evening as some kind of gracious cipher. 'Nothing's proven against him.'

He smiled rather patronisingly. 'In my view it's an open and shut case. But I shall be fair. We'll interview one of his supporters.' He looked straight into the eyes of Marie Leger. 'Your brother, Alain, for instance.'

'I'll come. Tomorrow.' She was suddenly brisk, businesslike. 'I don't want to be paid anything though.' Marie turned to her sister. 'Do you approve?' There was a genuine warmth in her voice.

'I don't know what to say – ' Mireille was disappointingly compromising, Annette thought.

'I think if I do take up the offer,' Marie said with the same briskness, 'it'll take some of the edge off my dislike for Alain.' She turned to Annette. 'I'm sure you'll understand; it's very hard to live in poverty when you *know* it's unjust. My sister is far more long-suffering and tolerant than I am. It's been years now, but I can't forget. And I can't forgive.' She paused and looked almost skittishly back at André. 'Of course, everything will very much depend on how much Monsieur Valier's lawyer lets me say, but I *am* grateful for the opportunity.'

André made a gallant little bow and the rest of the evening drained into innocuous small talk. After they had dropped the Leger sisters off and were driving back into St Esprit, Annette provoked the row that had been brooding for so long.

'You really are a bastard, aren't you?' she said. Quite suddenly she no longer cared about protecting their marriage.

'Thank you.'

'I had no idea you could behave that way.'

'You knew exactly what I wanted – and why the evening had been set up.' His voice was crisp and efficient, as if he realised the undercurrents of the past few months were now coming to a head.

'I just never realised how you'd manipulate her.'

But didn't she, Annette asked herself. Didn't she?

'I asked her straight out.'

'But why do you *want* to rake it all up?' Her words tumbled over each other.

'I'm not raking anything up. Surely you know what my responsibilities are – you've been married to them for long enough. A controversial man has been murdered. I need to reflect this. In as many words as I can. If this series is successful, then we can sell it to the nationals – overseas as well.'

But his logic finally pushed her over the top and she flashed out, 'You as good as killed Henri Larche anyway.'

'Really?'

'It was you who pursued this story, André, like you've never pursued anything before. It's been an obsession.'

'A campaign,' he corrected gently, reasonably.

'No, André. It's been an obsession. Why?'

He drew the car up outside their tall, unshuttered house. The windows looked bare, uninviting, almost threatening.

'Do shut up, Annette.'

'Just tell me – '

'I tell you – you're overtired, imagining things.'

'Why are you treating me like this?' She paused, almost breathless. 'Why are you so distant now?'

'It's all in the mind,' he said dismissively.

'Is it to do with no babies – no solutions to no babies?'

'I *must* get to bed. It's almost midnight,' André protested. He tried to put his arm round her but she pushed it away.

'Tell me.'

'There's nothing to tell.'

'Why were you after him? With such ferocity.'

André turned away. 'You're confused.'

'For God's sake – '

'I mean it. Somehow you're confusing us and him. If I'd known you were so worried about our marriage – '

'I'm worried about Henri Larche,' she protested vigorously, but she already felt a child in his hands and knew he was manipulating her.

'No. We must talk about us.'

'When?' she said eagerly and immediately felt angry. Now it looked as if she was clinging to some straw.

'Tomorrow.'

'When we've slept on it?' She laughed mockingly and wildly. 'Let's talk *now*.'

'I've got a newspaper to run in the morning.' He was edgy now and she felt a little surge of triumph.

'You never *stop* running the damn thing.'

He began to unlock the front door. As he did so someone emerged from the shadows somewhere further up the quiet, tree-lined road. He was walking slowly, absently. Annette and André turned to watch the night walker's progress.

'That's Marius Larche,' said André.

Marius was walking back to the house. Sleep had been an impossibility – probably still was, but he had had to try and tire himself somehow. Gabriel's words still resounded in his ears – father consorting with a top German officer. Why? And was it true? Or simply the understandable spite of a vicious old woman? But Gabriel seemed to have taken it seriously enough. He had tried to ring Alain but there had been no reply and eventually he had given up, walking the streets of St Esprit for hours. And as he had done so, the image of his father had disappeared to be replaced by another constant image – that of Natasha. He kept trying to see Monique – and failing. So Marius had gone on walking, almost twice round the town, and now, footsore, he was turning back.

Now he was walking uphill, and his pace quickened. Tomorrow. He would talk to his mother, sack Estelle, hire a cook, hire a nurse. Think about Alain's offer. Go and see Alain. Tonight – this morning – he would load himself with enough cognac to sleep.

So preoccupied were Marius' thoughts that he failed to

105

register the Claude dwelling as he drew near it, and he only paused because there was a light in the window and a car outside the house. He looked at his watch. Just after twelve-thirty. Perhaps Jean-Pierre was home, bailed and temporarily reprieved. Marius felt a pang of physical desire for him which quickly changed to guilt. He quickened his pace. Now he wanted to deaden feeling. The cognac would do that and the sooner he had it the better. His mind switched to his mother. He wondered how she was. Did he really trust that slut with her? He decided that he did. He must get up early tomorrow. Mother was at her best in the first hour of the morning. Later she would plunge almost totally into her own foggy world.

As he passed the small stone house, Marius stopped dead. The car. It was Gabriel's. Marius hesitated. So what if he's there, he thought. Probably he wanted to question him again. And Gabriel did not keep office hours. He made as if to walk on, but hesitated. Then he turned abruptly and cautiously walked back to peer in at the open window. The sound of the cicadas seemed to roar in his ears. Jean-Pierre was sitting down on a low, sagging chair. Gabriel had his hands on his shoulders. Marius doubled over in shock, his heart pounding, sweat pouring into his eyes.

8

Marius sat drinking his cognac, trying to clarify his thoughts. There seemed a strange intensity to the scene he had just witnessed. Why did Gabriel have his hands on Jean-Pierre's shoulders? Why was he there so late? Did he have some lead that he had not confided in Marius? Surely that was the most likely explanation? As he got drunker it all seemed to matter less. He was sitting in his father's study, surrounded by the dusty clutter, the accumulation of civic honour and small-town camaraderie. Marius could see him now, the tall emaciated figure at the desk. He remembered how he would turn to embrace him, those early mornings before school, the radiant Provençal light turning his dark hair and pink complexion to gold. His father had been like an old warrior, greeting his offspring, ruffling his hair and mouthing platitudes. But Marius had not wanted any of it, and he would soon fly to the warmth of his mother's embrace. Then, so quickly, his father had become an old man, turning the Château Letoric into his fortress where he had hidden, trapped and apprehensive.

Lured by the cognac, the tears came freely and he must have wept for a long time before he staggered up to bed. On the first landing there was the soft swish of what he muzzily thought was his father's dressing gown. But looking up he saw Estelle instead, wearing a filthy housecoat and hastily concealing a half-drunk bottle of his own whisky in one of the pockets.

'Monsieur.'

'Goodnight, Estelle.' He tried to stumble past her but she blocked his way.

'I must speak with you.' Her voice was as slurred as his and he almost laughed aloud. Two drunks and a mad old lady – the fall of the house of Larche.

'Can't it wait?'

'I must know where I stand.' She swayed slightly.

Marius sighed. 'Well?'

'How long will you be wanting me to stay in the house, monsieur?'

'I shall be hiring a nurse tomorrow,' Marius replied, trying to speak as clearly as possible. 'So if you could stay – '

'You'll never get one. Not to come here.'

'I'm going to an agency.'

'You'll still never get one. Not to come to this dump. Not after what happened.'

'Don't be absurd.'

'I bloody mean it.' She swayed slightly and he tried to push past her. Unfortunately Marius tripped and Estelle gave a great raucous laugh as he cannoned into her. 'Want a bit then?'

'Get out of the way.' He was mortified but panic overtook the mortification.

'Come on,' Estelle encouraged him. 'You need a break.'

'You're sacked,' he muttered.

'And *then* who's going to look after the old lady?' she said witheringly. 'We've had a nice quiet day – her and me. After that Alain Leger left. And by the way – when are you going to settle up?'

'Tomorrow morning.'

'Make sure you do.'

'And I'll give you another day's pay.'

'Might as well make it a week's – you won't get anyone. Besides, no one understands the old lady the way I do.'

'They can learn.' Marius succeeded in getting past her this time. She had obviously just had a bath. He could smell the expensive bath soap his father had liked. Suddenly he felt a wave of explosive hatred for her.

'Don't use my father's bathroom, his soap or – ' he looked meaningfully at the pocket of her housecoat – 'his drink.'

'In lieu of payment,' she replied truculently.

'You're being paid tomorrow – paid off.'

'I told you – you'll be lucky.'

'Go to hell.'

'What the hell do *you* want?'

'Something's come up.'

Jean-Pierre Claude pulled the window a little further up. He blinked in the early morning sunlight. The lavender field stretched out hazily blue in front of him.

'It's barely six.'

'It won't wait. You'll regret it if you don't hear what I have to say.'

'My mother – '

'Come out of the window. Then you won't wake her up.'

'I'll get dressed.'

'Hurry.'

He dragged on a pair of filthy jeans, socks, boots and a sweater. Then, wheezing slightly, Jean-Pierre Claude clambered over the window sill.

The phone rang at Marius' bedside just after six a.m. And he woke with a considerable start, confusing the sound with his alarm clock and reaching out to switch it off. When this proved ineffective he sat up, realising that the unwelcome sound was someone trying to reach him.

'Yes?'

'It's me.'

'Who?' He yawned blearily.

'It's Monique.'

Marius looked at his watch. 'Something wrong?'

'No. I realise it's early – I just couldn't sleep.'

'So there *is* something wrong.'

'Well – ' She paused unhappily. 'I was very understanding when you phoned. I meant to be.' Monique paused again. 'I mean to be.'

'But you find it hard,' said Marius gently but wearily. He should have realised that she had taken it all too well.

'Yes.'

'Too hard?'

109

'No – Marius – when are we going to get married?'

'When this is over.'

'It could drag on for months,' she said with conviction. 'We must have a deadline.'

'For the end of this investigation?' He attempted to joke, knowing that he was wrong to try from the moment he opened his mouth.

'Don't be a fool – I want us to marry now. In a fortnight.'

'Monique – '

'Or not at all.'

'What are you frightened of?' he asked almost irritably.

'I want us together. Making a fresh start.'

'Do you think I could have AIDS?' Marius spoke softly and she asked him to repeat what he had said, although he was sure she had heard the first time.

'I pray you haven't. But – '

'I haven't. I've had – checks.'

There was a long silence.

'Do you trust me?' he asked.

More silence.

'Do you trust me?'

'It's not trust. You can't help your own inclinations.' Her voice was steady, unwavering.

'If I marry you – '

'If?'

'When I marry you, I assure you there'll be no more Jean-Pierre Claudes.'

'I know you mean that.'

'But you don't believe me,' Marius said sadly.

'I just want us to be married – not to put you under lock and key – but so I can love you – really mean something to you. Day by day. So I must hold you to this deadline.'

'You mean fourteen days is unnegotiable?' asked Marius.

'It shouldn't have to be.'

'I don't want it to be,' he said quietly.

'Are you sure?' Monique was hesitant.

'Of course I'm damn well sure.'

'You won't let me come down?'

'How can you? The house is in chaos.' He was very firm. 'But I'll ring you, my darling. And I'll marry you in fourteen days.'

110

There was no more to be said and after their goodbyes, Marius put the phone down and then sat for a long time with his head in his hands. He wanted to do as she said, but her world seemed to be in another dimension from his own.

Marius made coffee at seven and took a cup up to his mother. It was another depressingly perfect morning and the roses on the terrace gave off a heady perfume. He had a slight hangover – one that he could cope with – and even the thought of last night's encounter with Estelle did not entirely make him despair, despite the fact that he knew she was probably right. And then, of course, there was his recent conversation with Monique. His head buzzed with trepidation and a sense of unreality gripped him. Officially he only had another ten days' vacation in which to think. Perhaps he should seriously consider putting his mother into a nursing home, but it would take time to select one and again what about the cost? He still favoured the nurse – as long as it wasn't too expensive and essentially it wasn't Estelle.

'Mother.'

He heard the slight moaning noise she made in the early morning and opened the door. Solange lay on her back, her eyes blankly open, her large moon face devoid of expression. As always, Marius felt part tender pity, part wonderment that his mysterious and glamorous and alluring mother could be reduced to this. Her hands were about the only part of her body that had not changed. They were long, tapering – still the hands of a young woman, unmarked by the brown age spots that raddled her face. Suddenly, Marius remembered those hands stroking his face as a child when they had visited the Anne Frank house in Amsterdam. His mother had been deeply moved in the house, particularly by the faded scrap-book cuttings that were still lovingly preserved under perspex on the equally faded wall – the icons of Anne's imprisonment, fantasy film-star glimpses of an exotic outside world.

'Mother.'

'Mm.' Was she mentally coherent, or not?

'How did you sleep?'

'I don't think I did.'

111

'What have you been doing all night?' His voice was very gentle.

'Thinking of Henri.'

'In what way?'

'How happy we were.'

'All those rumours . . .' He felt bad now, trying to grill her at the most likely time.

'What rumours?'

'Nothing. What – were you thinking of the happy times?'

'They were all happy times.'

'Even the war?'

'It was dangerous.'

'And Henri?'

'Henri?'

'Was he in danger?'

She nodded.

'Who from?'

She shook her head.

'Not Kummel?'

Solange was very still.

'Did he know him?'

She said nothing.

'Mother – '

'He got information from Kummel.' Her voice was sing-song but he was sure that she had understood what he had asked her – and was equally sure that she was telling him the truth. 'Occasionally.'

'I thought Father was outside the Maquis?'

'He was. It was just Kummel – Kummel he spoke to.' She spoke childishly, but the simple statement gave Marius hope. He was also sweating with apprehension for although his mother was giving him information – vital information – would she ever remember it again? Did he have a tape-recorder? Somewhere? But he knew he didn't. She was getting restless now, her hands were plucking at the counterpane.

'Mother, how many times did Father see this man?'

'I don't know. Henri – I don't know.'

'It's Marius, Mother.'

'You told me – you told me, Henri. You told us all. Alain. You told him.' She was mumbling.

112

'Did Alain meet Kummel too?'

'So what's next, darling?'

'Next?'

'Where are you going to take me today, Henri? Shall we go out for lunch?'

'Where would you like to go?' asked Marius, ready to humour her.

'To the café by the river.'

'Le Clozel?'

'I want to go there with Henri and Wolfgang. They never take me. Of course – it belongs to them now. To the Nazis.'

'The café?'

'The coffee. They took all my coffee.'

'Mother, I brought you some.'

'No.' She was getting very agitated now, sitting bolt upright in bed, fingers pulling at the sheets. 'They took my coffee.'

'It's here.'

Marius offered it to her but before he could react, she punched the air and caught the saucer. Coffee leapt in an arc towards her, splashing her nightgown and the sheets. Solange set up a howl of childish rage which quickly turned to an animal cry of drawn-out lament.

'Mother – it's only coffee.'

She howled louder.

'Mother – '

'Now what's going on?' It was Estelle, framed in the doorway, her face greasy with night cream and smelling of whisky.

'She punched at the saucer and – '

'She must have been upset.'

'We were having a chat.'

'What about?'

'None of your business,' yelled Marius above his mother's cries. He thoroughly resented Estelle's tone. It was as if she was taking over in his own house. But wasn't it his own fault for neglecting his mother, he admitted honestly.

'She's thoroughly upset.' Estelle went up to her. 'Quieten down, my lovely. Estelle's here now. She'll look after you.'

Solange subsided a little, but pointed an accusing finger at Marius.

'It's him.'

113

'What's he done?' asked Estelle with pleased vindictiveness.

'He's from the Boche,' pronounced Solange, gesturing at her son. 'Bloody Hun.'

Marius walked down the stairs and out on to the terrace, cursing. Then he went back inside, picked up the telephone receiver, looked at his watch, shrugged and dialled Monique's number. She answered after it had rung over a dozen times.

'Yes?'

'It's Marius.'

'Darling – I'm sorry. I was asleep – I'm so tired.'

'Shall I ring back?'

'I just wanted to reassure you. About the deadline. You're on?'

'I thought I'd pressured you into it?'

'No.'

'Why can't I come down? Today. Share it with you.'

'No.'

'Marius – '

'Please. No. I'll be with you soon. I – I just want to talk. I must get rid of Estelle.'

'Let *me* come. I can – '

'No.'

'Marius, *why* won't you let me help?'

'Because I don't want you mixed up in this filthy business, that's all.'

'It won't go away. It won't be over in a fortnight. Not just like that.'

'I know.'

'So what are you going to do?' Her voice was edgy.

'I have to get rid of her. She's practically taken Mother over – and she's incredibly rude to me.'

'I'd keep her.' Monique's voice was firm.

'You're exhausted. Your father's been *murdered*, Marius. How *can* you think straight? But you'll never get a nurse in – not in these circumstances. And if Estelle's reliable – is she?'

'With my mother – yes.'

'Offer her a decent salary. Make her responsible.'

Marius stood thinking about it. The employment of Estelle

was an unpalatable thought, but if she lived in until he had properly considered Alain's plan . . .

'Marius?'

'I'm here.'

'Well?'

'Maybe you're right. Temporarily.' His voice was hollow.

'I know she's a pain. But you won't be *there* – don't you see?'

'Yes, I see. But Alain – Alain Leger. He's offering to go into partnership with me, to restore Letoric. Maybe, then, we could get a nurse to live in.'

'That's a wonderful offer.'

'I'm thinking it over.'

'And can Estelle cope in the mean time?'

'Yes,' said Marius slowly. 'I think she can cope.' The question is, he thought, can I? Again they said their goodbyes – and again he sat for a long time with his head in his hands.

Mariola Claude lifted herself heavily and arthritically out of her bed.

'Jean-Pierre,' she croaked. He wasn't a bad boy always, she thought. Sometimes, just sometimes, he made his old mother a cup of coffee in the morning. And surely she deserved it today of all days. After all, it was on the surety of her property that he had got bail. And where was he? In bed, no doubt, snoring his head off. Well, at least he hadn't had anything to drink last night – Rodiet had brought him back too late for that. She supposed he had stayed questioning him for hours. Certainly they had been hard at it when she'd gone to bed. So maybe she'd let him off. For once.

Mariola clutched her nightdress to her and ambled into her son's room.

'Jean-Pierre.'

The sheets were pushed back and the window was open. A breeze rustled some rolled-up cigarette papers on the scarred card table in the corner.

'Jean-Pierre.'

Mariola moved slowly to the window and looked out. She could see him sitting on the old tractor on the rutted track beside the lavender field.

115

'Jean-Pierre,' she shouted again, but he didn't turn towards her.

'Estelle.'

'Yes, monsieur?'

'Can you come into the study for a moment?'

'Of course.'

For the first time in months she was quite well dressed. Her linen skirt had been well ironed and her blouse looked crisp and fresh. She had obviously just bathed and washed her hair, but this time he couldn't smell his father's bath soap on her.

'I want to talk to you.'

'I'm sorry I said what I did.'

'That's all right.' Marius paused and looked out of the window. It was nine and the sun was high in a cobalt sky. 'Look – you're right about the nurse. Can we strike a bargain?'

'Yes, monsieur?' She looked up at him, grinning. The old Estelle was back, but only temporarily. Her coquettish look vanished in seconds.

'You keep to the house rules, and I'll employ you.'

'And what are the house rules?'

'Keep off the drink and behave responsibly to my mother. And if you will – you can take over as nurse and housekeeper.'

'What will you pay me?' she asked flatly.

He mentioned a sum, and she nodded. 'Did you expect as much?' he asked.

But she didn't reply. Then she said slowly, 'I'm fond of the old lady. I'll look after her. But for how long?'

'Until she becomes unmanageable.' Or Alain and I can make other arrangements, he thought.

'And then?'

'We'll have to think again. It's a big responsibility, but I'm paying you well. Is there anyone at home?'

She shook her head.

'So you'll live in?'

'If I can have a better bedroom. At the moment I'm camping in her dressing-room.'

'Take your pick. I shall be going back to Lyon in ten days' time. Of course I'll be in contact. Every day, on the phone. And obviously I shall visit much more frequently,' he added and caught the look of understanding in her eyes. She knows I'll be checking up on her, he thought. Alain, too – I'm sure he'll keep tabs on her.

'Very well, monsieur. I'll try. But as the old lady becomes – '

'I know – I've told you. I'll make a decision about that. What are you staring at?'

Her gaze was fixed rigidly on the window. 'It's Mariola – Mariola Claude. She's coming up the drive. And I've never seen her move so fast in her life.'

Marius spun round. Estelle was right. Mariola Claude was staggering up the weed-choked gravel, her face working. And she was shouting something. It was only when she had almost reached the front door that he could make out what it was.

'Murder!' she was screaming. 'Murder!'

9

'Yes?' Marius opened the front door, standing on the threshold, his skin icy against his cotton trousers and shirt. 'What do you want?'

But she was babbling incoherently.

'Madame – what do you want? What's the matter?'

Estelle pushed past him and took her gently by the shoulders. Marius was reminded of what he had seen last night – Gabriel taking Jean-Pierre by the shoulders so intently. But Mariola Claude was still gibbering incoherently. Then she whispered the word again.

'Murder.'

'Who's been murdered?' asked Estelle with a warmth that Marius had not noticed in her before. She was obviously good with old ladies. But what did she mean by murder? Marius knew he was not registering, but the same icy feeling was with him.

'Jean-Pierre,' she said and then repeated his name. 'Jean-Pierre.'

'Murder?' asked Marius dully.

'They cut his throat,' she said.

They both stared at her uncomprehendingly. Then the professional in Marius swung into action. 'Where is he?'

'On the tractor.'

'And he's *dead*?'

'They cut his throat.'

'They?'

'Whoever it is. They did for your father. Now they've done for my boy. My son.' She rocked herself to and fro, incoherently muttering again.

'I'll go,' said Marius. 'Phone the police and then look after her here.'

Estelle nodded.

A breeze stirred the lavender field and Marius inhaled the scent from its soft, musky blooms. From somewhere, a long way away, came the distant sound of a transistor radio. With a jolt, he could see the figure of Jean-Pierre sitting in the seat of the ancient blue tractor. He was slumped forward, his head on the steering wheel, and Marius could see a cluster of flies, swooping and diving around him.

Rather than feeling shocked or revolted, Marius was flooded with compassion. As he drew level with Jean-Pierre, he could see the blood. As with his father, there was an amazing amount of it, hidden by the rusty dashboard, over the engine housing of the tractor and down to a shiny pool on the ground.

Jean-Pierre's eyes stared ahead in minute examination of the steering wheel, and his hands drooped by his side. His face had set in a rigid expression of astonishment. Marius reached out and stroked his bare arm. It was still warm, or was it the sun that was now high and blazing in the sky? Ineffectually clapping his hands Marius tried to disperse the flies, but they returned in seconds. Some of them clustered around Jean-Pierre's vacant, open eyes.

Who the hell has done this? he wondered. What did Jean-Pierre know that warranted this barbaric act? While the motive for his father's murder still seemed obvious, this one was inexplicable. His memory flashed back to the scene he had witnessed last night: Gabriel with his hands on Jean-Pierre's shoulders, looking down at him so intently. What did it mean? An interrogation? A warning?

Again his hand stroked the warm brown flesh of Jean-Pierre's arm. Then Marius realised that he was having an erection. God, he was being excited by a dead man. But Marius felt no sense of shame. He went on stroking Jean-Pierre's arm and remembering the times when he had turned to him, the times when they had both turned to each other – way behind and beyond the days of bitterness and blackmail and regret.

'Jean-Pierre,' he whispered. 'Remember?' And Marius remembered for them both.

The yearning, the lavender fields, the sunflowers – all merged into one, each one part of the same. The heat on Jean-Pierre's clumsy bronzed body. Marius reached out – they both reached out and their limbs met, straining against each other, locked against each other. So many times he had said to himself it would be the last. But it had never been. Had he loved him, or just lusted after him? Were the two synonymous? He continued to stroke Jean-Pierre's arm, his erection hard against his trousers.

'Monsieur Larche.'

'Who?' Marius spun round. 'Ah – ' He was confused, horrified, as if he had been caught fornicating. It was Lebatre, looking heavily commanding.

'They called me – your girl . . .'

'Estelle.'

Lebatre edged nearer. 'What a lot of blood,' he said absently.

'Yes.'

'The same method – '

'As my father.'

'We've got a psychopath on the loose,' Lebatre said stiffly.

'Same motive, perhaps?'

'Hardly. Perhaps he knew something. But what? Your father was killed for revenge. What was Claude killed for?'

'We don't know what my father was killed for,' said Marius slowly. 'In the light of what's happened, maybe the motive wasn't revenge.'

'Then what the hell was it?'

'Perhaps my father knew something. And Jean-Pierre knew it too.'

'Pure speculation,' snapped Lebatre.

'Absolutely,' admitted Marius. 'Is Gabriel coming out?'

'He's been told. But there's no *reason* for him to come – *I'm* in charge of this case.' His voice was defensive.

'Gabriel brought Jean-Pierre back last night.'

'Why?' Lebatre sounded very surprised.

'Don't ask me.'

'I said we'd finished with him and could he get one of the men at the Gendarmerie to bring him back.'

120

'Well, he didn't.'

'How do you know?'

'I saw them through the window. Talking.'

Lebatre frowned and spoke quietly. 'He had no right.'

'Sorry?'

'He shouldn't interfere. It was my case. So is this. Just because
. . .' He paused.

'Because what?' asked Marius curiously.

'It's local, isn't it? Amongst friends.'

'Well . . .'

'That's why he's interfering.'

'Aren't you being rather unprofessional?' Marius' tone was
sharp.

Lebatre shrugged. 'I'm reacting as any man would.'

'Any *police*man?'

Lebatre shrugged again and there was an awkward pause.
Abruptly he changed the subject. 'I've got the forensic team
coming out here.' He looked at his watch. 'They won't be long.'

'Well?'

'It's a rerun.'

Gabriel shrugged. His team surrounded Jean-Pierre, still
slumped over his tractor wheel but now the object of much
attention. He was being photographed, dusted for fingerprints
and carefully scrutinised by the doctor who had already pulled
his stiffening body forward to examine the sharp slit in his
neck. Lebatre supervised a team searching the arid, straggling
undergrowth and the sun beat down relentlessly on everyone.

'We can't take that for granted.'

'Two different killers in such a short space of time. Unlikely.'

'I never rule anything out, Marius.'

'Do you suspect me?'

'After your confession?'

'Come on, Gabriel. I could have hated him.'

'I saw him last night. I know what you thought of him.'

'How?'

'He told me. Even a very temporary abstinence seemed to
have clarified his mind.'

'What did he tell you?'

121

'He told me how fond he was of you – and how sorry he'd been about those blackmail notes. He claimed to have written them very much under the influence.'

Marius nodded. 'That's probably true.'

'Then he told me that however much he provoked you, you would still be very fond of him.'

'You believed him?'

'He spoke genuinely.'

'Come on, Gabriel. You're being unprofessional.' He was accusing Rodiet now, just as he had accused Lebatre.

'No, I'm acting on my experience of human beings.'

'I saw you with him last night.'

'In the car?' He appeared completely unruffled.

'In the house. I'd been walking – and I saw you both through the window.' Marius paused. 'I was surprised.'

'Surprised?'

'That you'd brought him home – that you hadn't left it to one of your minions.'

'I wanted to talk to him. I'm very interested in this case, Marius. It's my roots.'

'Lebatre is furious,' said Marius reprovingly.

'I did notice a certain coolness.'

'Don't you care?'

'Not a lot. He's a boor.'

'So you'll go on – taking an interest?'

'I shall.'

'What else did Jean-Pierre talk to you about? You seemed to be having a very intense conversation. When I looked in he was sitting in a chair and you were holding his shoulders. Pressing him down.'

'He got very emotional.'

'What about?' They were sparring now; instinctively Marius was convinced of it, although at the same time his reason told him that his imagination could be playing him false.

'You. He regretted very much what he had done.'

'Because he was in trouble with the police?'

'Because of what he had done to you.'

Marius looked at the brown arm, getting rigid now as it hung over the tractor. Suddenly he wanted to touch it again. To find out if it had gone cold.

'Gabriel, I have to stay. I have to stay and talk to people.'

'I warned you to keep out of this.'

'You also asked me to make a few enquiries – unofficially.'

'That's over. I've decided I was wrong.'

Gabriel looked towards his busy team, still attending to the dead man.

'Do you need me here any longer?' said Marius abruptly.

'Where will you be?'

'I'll be at home for the rest of the morning,' he replied sharply.

'OK. I'll keep you informed.' Gabriel turned back to his team, briskly efficient. 'And I shall need to know your movements last night.'

'That's easy,' said Marius. 'I got drunk and went to sleep. You can ask Estelle.'

He walked slowly away, taking a last look at that brown arm. But it suddenly didn't look like an arm any longer – just like the plastic limb of some outsize, broken, bloodied doll.

'Welcome.'

She stepped self-consciously into André Valier's office. It was curiously stark and functional. Marie Leger had expected some kind of Hollywood news reporter sleaze; she had almost had him in eye-shade and pinned shirt-sleeves. Instead there was a large, clear desk, a fax machine, a sleek telephone, a book-case containing the complete works of Zola, and a deep-pile carpet. There were some Seurat prints on the walls and, on a glass table, an exquisite china shepherd boy playing a flute.

André was dressed in a linen suit with a cream shirt and light blue tie. There was a coolness to him that was almost mocking and Marie, never confident, always defensive, felt instantly threatened. She was sure that some part of him was laughing at her.

'Do sit down.'

There was a metal chair covered in black leather on one side of the desk. It matched the other on which André was sitting. He smiled at her. Like a cat with cream, she thought.

'There's been a development.'

'Yes?' she asked, startled.

123

'You haven't heard? Jean-Pierre Claude – he's been found with his throat cut. Sitting on his tractor.'

'God – '

'Looks like a serial killer.'

'What do you mean?'

'Repeated murders. With more to come.' His voice had an obscene relish to it.

'This is terrible. It must be some dreadful maniac.'

'Or someone who's anxious – very anxious indeed – to keep people quiet.'

'Quiet about what?' Marie was obviously deeply shocked.

André shrugged. The little smile was still on his lips. Is he playing a game with me, she wondered. And, if so, what sort of game is it? 'I've been wondering if the Larche killing wasn't just revenge. Perhaps the old man knew something – about someone. And so did Claude. And maybe others.'

'Then there could be more of these killings . . .'

'Maybe.'

'But what is it – what could they have known?'

'Maybe Henri Larche didn't preside over that – tribunal. Maybe it was someone else.' His teasing smile broadened. 'Maybe these killings have been done by someone trying to protect someone else – or someone trying to protect themselves.'

'They must be mad,' she replied expressionlessly.

'Perhaps they are.' He got up and went outside. 'I'll be back in a minute.' Marie watched him walk down a long, grubby corridor. He opened a door and there was a bustle of sound – a sharp contrast to the quiet of his own neat eyrie. But in seconds he was back, holding the front page of a newspaper. Hold the front page. That's what they said in the films – the old films she sometimes watched on Sunday afternoon television in winter. He strode towards her and slapped it down on his pristine desk. The banner headline ran: SERIAL KILLER AT WORK? And then in only slightly smaller black lettering: MURDERED LABOUR-ER'S LINK TO LARCHE. Bemused she read on:

The body of farm labourer Jean-Pierre Claude was found this morning slumped on a tractor. His throat had been cut. This is the second killing in the St Esprit area in days. Police Commissaire

124

Gabriel Rodiet stated this morning: 'I really can't say whether these killings are linked or not.' However both men had their throats cut and were killed in the same way.

She looked up. 'I don't know anything about the tribunal,' she said abruptly.

'But you were in St Esprit during the occupation.'

'As a young girl. Yes. But all we knew was what we read in the papers.'

'Are you sure about that, madame?'

'Quite sure.'

'And your sister?'

'She knows nothing either. Ask her.'

'I shall,' said André crisply.

'So you'll not want me now.' She half stood up but he waved her down again.

'What makes you think that?' he asked quietly.

'Well – there have been new developments – '

'We're still interested in running stories on Henri Larche.'

'Stories?' she asked hesitantly. 'You mean you've got others – other people to write things?'

He shifted in his chair slightly and she realised that this was the first time she had seen André Valier even slightly disconcerted. 'Perhaps.'

'May I know who they are?'

'Let's talk about what I'd like you to write first.'

'Very well.' Marie cursed herself for giving in to him.

'The question of the house – and your brother. How did this come about?'

She was silent and he wondered if she was going to reply. 'My father died without making a will,' she said suddenly, 'so it seemed logical that we should share the estate. Then Henri Larche produced some absurd document; they said it was a letter of intent my father had written him. Anyway, it was sufficient for my brother Alain to inherit – and for us to live in poverty.'

'When did he produce this document?'

'Just after the war. In 1947.'

'And that was that?'

'We disputed it, of course. Naturally.'

'And?'

125

'And we lost. Then we lost the appeal. Then we moved out to that damn cottage and we've been there ever since. Living in quiet penury – eking out a small income with the shop.'

'You're still angry?'

'Very. He obviously felt we were unfit to manage the estate'.

'Do you speak to your brother?'

'No. I suppose he imagined we'd sell for holiday homes.'

'Does he try to speak to you?'

'He makes overtures sometimes, but we don't encourage them.'

'Is your sister as bitter as you?'

'No, she's more philosophical.' Marie sighed. He must know some – or all – of this.

'Well now.' He leant back in his chair. 'Will you write all this down for me?'

'I'm not sure that I can. And I don't know the legal position.'

He looked impatient. 'You can tell the story to a reporter. And I'll have a lawyer clear everything. We need to focus on your memories of Larche. As a man. Then as a manipulator. Did you know Claude?'

'I know his mother. He was – very uncouth, I think.'

'Maybe he looked it.'

'What do you mean?'

'False impressions?' There was a trace of contempt in André's eyes.

'If you really want to know – he was a drunk,' she said sharply, pursing her lips and feeling ridiculous, knowing the conversation was being forced on her. Suddenly Marie felt not just confused but utterly wretched. Hadn't this been a chance to publicly rebuke Alain – the much older brother who had been so distant when she was a child and then had swooped in like a vulture to take everything she and Mireille should have shared. The other object of her hatred was dead. And she had been pleased – knew she had been pleased. It was what he deserved.

But she stood up abruptly. 'I don't know whether I should be doing this.' Again she cursed herself; why didn't she just walk out, telling him and his scurrilous article to go to bloody hell? But she was just too indecisive to do it. A wave of faintness swept over her as she swung between distaste for his methods and an unwelcome awareness that for far too long she herself

126

had fed off the same scurrilousness that André Valier practised in his newspaper.

'Please – don't upset yourself.' Valier also stood up, all instant ingenuous concern. 'I think you're – '

'No I'm not.'

'I'm sorry?'

Finally she had the right words – the right feelings. Marie looked straight at him for the first time. And as the contempt for him welled up in her, the courage came too. It was an exhilarating release. If she could do this, she wondered, then why couldn't she throw her other scheme up too? But, wearily, she knew she wouldn't. It had been going on too long, she was so very implicated – and there was so much money at stake.

'Monsieur Valier, you are a total bastard.'

He gazed at her, mouth agape, the little smile wiped off his face. Marie almost laughed aloud with triumph and derision.

'Of course I'm a foolish and embittered woman. Of course I am.' She paused. 'I wanted to see Alain squirm. But what are you trying to do? Boost circulation? Or does it give you pleasure to stir up these old quarrels again?'

'You're upset.' His voice was soothing but she could see something in his eyes – a kind of recognition.

'No. I'm seeing my own despicable actions clearly for the first time – and finding the guts to voice them. I'm not writing a word for your scurrilous little tabloid. I know what you'll say – that this is investigative journalism. Rubbish. It's pure shit. Yes, you can look surprised. An ageing spinster like me capable of thinking like this – talking like this. But at last I've found the – the spirit to say what I feel. And I'm grateful to you. There are plenty of people in this town who will write for you for money, monsieur. Plenty of scandal-mongers. But don't count me amongst them.' She gazed at him with contempt. 'God damn you, Valier,' she said quietly. 'You don't deserve the wife you have. I saw her looking away from you last night at dinner. She must loathe and despise your manipulations.' Marie walked towards the door. She was amazed at herself – amazed at what she was saying. Marie opened the door and stood there inconclusively. 'Go to hell,' she said at last.

*

As Marie walked through the rather dingy foyer with its air conditioning humming and its dim light a protection against the heat outside, she suddenly paused. Sitting in the reception area were Estelle and Madame Claude. She was about to hurry on, but then she became aware that the old woman's eyes were fixed on her. Reluctantly she went across.

'Madame Claude, I am so terribly sorry.'

But the old woman shook her head impatiently. 'I've come to be interviewed.' She made the statement with a kind of triumphant misery, as if some drama of her own had to be played out in contrast to the existing drama of her son's slashed throat.

'Are you sure that's wise?' Marie glanced at Estelle who returned the look with a hostile stare.

'Yes. I want to give a statement.'

'What about?'

'His murder. You see – I know who did it.' She began to shake and Estelle put a reassuring hand on her shoulder.

'Don't say any more,' she whispered. But Madame Claude was determined not to miss her chance.

'It was that little cunt of a nancy boy,' she shouted, pleased at Marie's shocked expression. 'I've come to expose him. That bastard Larche.'

'She's beside herself. You should take her home.'

'How can I? We were brought out here by car.' Estelle for once looked genuinely frightened.

'By car?'

'Valier sent it for us.'

'You should take her home. I'll drive you.'

'I'll never shift her now,' said Estelle.

'I'm not moving,' retorted the old woman loudly, causing everyone in the foyer to turn and stare at her curiously. 'Not till I've said what I have to say. It was that poofter Larche. He killed my son. Like he killed his own father. He was making advances to my dearest – ' She began to cry in hoarse, dry sobs. 'And Jean-Pierre – he wasn't having any. So Larche cut his throat.'

'But why should he cut his father's throat?'

'Jealousy. Money. I don't know.' The old woman was frantic now and her words were lost amid hysterical sobs.

Marie glanced back at Estelle. 'I thought you were meant to be looking after Madame Larche – that's what I heard.'

'You heard right. But her son's with her now. I told him I had to have some time off.'

'And this is how you're spending it?' demanded Marie censoriously.

'It's none of your business.'

'And is he paying Madame Claude?'

'He'll pay,' muttered the old woman. 'That whore of a Larche will pay.'

'Good morning.' A young secretary, bright and brisk in a crisp suit, stood beside them. 'Madame Claude?'

'Yes, this is Madame Claude,' said Estelle, relieved.

'Thank you for coming. Monsieur Valier will see you both now.'

'Just a minute,' said Marie.

All their eyes turned on her questioningly.

'Yes?' asked the secretary, a little less brightly.

'Will you give a message to Monsieur Valier for me?'

'And you are?' She looked puzzled now.

'Madame Leger. I've just been with him.'

'Oh yes – '

'Tell him – tell him that he's an absolute, unmitigated swine.'

'I beg your – ' The secretary flushed scarlet.

'Yes,' chimed in Madame Claude in her blurred voice. 'That's what he is – that Larche. But swine's too good for him. He's a – '

She was led away muttering by Estelle and the flustered secretary amidst the outright curiosity and fascination of everyone in the foyer of the *Journal Discours*.

Marie watched them go and then turned miserably towards the swing doors and the torpid heat. Despite everything that had happened to her, Marie Leger felt she had never fully realised what a wicked place the world was. But she knew that she couldn't give up now. She had too much at stake. As she walked out into the glare of the harsh sunlight, a radical thought crossed her mind. Why not give up? Why not go straight to Rodiet and tell him what she and Jean-Pierre had really been doing? It was a sudden, wonderful, seductive temptation. But quite hopeless. And besides – there was the money she was owed. Marie realised that what she was doing was far worse than Valier could ever do. But that didn't make her any less contemptuous of him.

'Alain?' Marius' voice was hesitant on the telephone.

'Yes, Marius?'

'Can we talk?'

'Come to lunch.' He sounded wonderfully calm and reassuring.

'Have you heard what's happened?'

'I've heard nothing. I don't think I want to hear anything else.'

'Jean-Pierre's been murdered.'

'No – '

'Throat cut. Just like Father.'

There was a long pause. Then Alain said slowly, 'Do they know who did it?'

'No. Lebatre's technically in charge with Rodiet interfering.'

'Why the *hell* has this happened?'

'That's what they would like to know. Meanwhile I'm one of their principal suspects.'

Alain laughed emptily. 'Absurd.'

'Gabriel seems to share that view. But Lebatre – '

'I can have lunch ready by twelve thirty.'

'I'll be there then. But – before I ring off – did *you* ever meet Kummel?'

'No. Why should I?'

'My father was seen lunching with him.'

'By whom?'

'Mariola Claude.'

'She's not a reliable witness,' he replied quietly, abruptly.

'Supposing she's right?'

'There's nothing sinister about the old woman being right. Henri probably lunched with him to pump for information.'

'That's what my mother said. But wouldn't you have *known* that my father lunched with Kummel? You were both so close.'

'I just can't remember the actual episode. But if he *did* lunch with him, maybe he gave whatever information he got to your

130

mother. And maybe she thought if too many people knew . . .'
He stopped impatiently. 'Anyway, it's all conjecture.'

There was another long pause. Then Marius said, 'She *is* unreliable. Isn't she?'

'Mariola Claude? She's a very embittered woman who was knocked around by her husband – just like her son was. She's never had a penny to her name, and she's addicted to gossip.' He broke off. 'Now look – come up here and we'll talk.'

'Estelle, are you back?'

'Yes.' She was standing in the hallway, looking beaten.

'I'm going out to – what's the matter? Where's Madame Claude?'

'She's with the police now – with Lebatre.'

'Still there? I thought that by now . . .' Marius looked at her in bewilderment. 'You've been gone for ages,' he accused.

'I took her into Aix.'

'What?'

'Valier phoned. He wanted to interview her.'

'But you told me you had to help Madame Claude while she was with the police.'

'I lied.'

Marius gazed at her in silence, stunned by her frankness.

'You're doing something very stupid,' he shouted, but then, remembering his mother, lowered his voice to a bitter, steely note. 'You're a – '

'Before you begin to abuse me, monsieur, I have something to tell you.'

'I don't want to hear it.'

'You should. It affects you.'

'Well?'

'Yes, you're right. I was a fool to go. Not because of the money – I needed it and I'd do it again. However, it's unlikely I'll get the chance.'

'What are you trying to say?'

'I'm trying to say the old lady was more crazy than I thought – and the shock has made her crazier. She made a scene in the foyer of the newspaper – and an even bigger one in Valier's office.'

131

'What kind of scene?'

'Shouting. Making accusations.'

'What kind of accusations?'

'They were about you.' She looked at him wildly. 'Saying you'd murdered her son.'

'I see.' A wave of appalling fatigue hit Marius. 'And what did Valier say?'

'Not a lot. He could see how unbalanced she was – and there was nothing he could print.'

'He must have been disappointed.'

'He was.'

'And then what happened?'

'He told me to take her away. So I did – to the police. She told me Lebatre wanted to see her this morning. He must have phoned her. So we came back here by taxi – at my expense.'

Marius stared at her. 'Why are you telling me all this?'

'You should know.' She turned away. 'And believe it or not, I was ashamed. I'm not often ashamed. I felt dirty – playing into his hands, accepting his money. I'd rather screw him. Any time. And now I suppose you'll sack me.'

'How can I?' asked Marius with sudden, ironic humour. 'I need you too much – and you damn well know it. Don't you?'

Estelle nodded, but without triumph.

10

'You're a fool, Marie.'

'Yes.'

The Leger sisters sat outside their house on the terrace that they both considered was the only good thing about their small home. The tiny garden was entirely enclosed by a mellow stone wall, high enough to prevent them from being overlooked but not so high that it made them feel claustrophobic. The air was pungent with the scent of late wallflowers from Mireille's tubs and the herbs that Marie had allowed to grow between the paving stones.

It was lunchtime. Mireille had just returned from the shop and they were eating an oiled salad with cheese and fresh bread.

'At least you admit it.'

'I'm grateful to Valier,' said Marie. 'Grateful that he made me angry enough to see what I was doing.'

Mireille looked at her sister curiously. 'I really think you've changed,' she said. 'Perhaps it needed – all this stupidity.'

'Perhaps it did. Mariola tells me there's a man who knows things – who the police don't know about. Someone called Didier. Jean-Pierre was seeing him.' Marie calculated the effect of what she had just said on her sister.

'Where?'

'He's in an asylum – a psychiatric hospital.'

'He's mad then?'

'He's meant to be.'

'And the police don't know about him?'

'No. Not yet.'

'Then they should.'

'Yes . . .' Marie paused indecisively.

'Is Mariola going to tell them? And why was Jean-Pierre seeing him?'

'I don't know.'

'Mariola is a cunning old woman. You should never have got mixed up with her in the first place,' said Mireille severely. 'If she's told you something – you have a duty to tell the police.'

'I don't want to do that.' She hesitated.

'Marie, what's going on?'

'Nothing.' She cut her cheese into tiny methodical squares.

'I know that look,' insisted Mireille. 'You're hiding something from me.'

'No.'

'What *is* it?'

Then Marie blurted out: 'She doesn't know.'

'Who?'

'Mariola – she doesn't know I went to see Didier too.'

'You *what*?'

'I went with Jean-Pierre.' Now at least some of it was coming out. Marie felt an elation she had never experienced before. But the question was – would she eventually tell everything? Could she? Her visits to Didier were merely the tip of an iceberg.

'What in God's name for?'

Marie's voice shook. 'We had this plan.'

Mireille had stood up. She was trembling. 'What have you done?' she whispered. Her face was grey. 'What kind of plan could you have had with the likes of him?'

'We thought Didier could confirm that Henri did it – that he presided over that court.'

'And did he?'

'No.'

'So – what *did* he say?'

'I can't tell you.'

'You *must*.'

'No. I don't want to think about it again. It's of no importance.'

Mireille came and stood over her threateningly and for a moment Marie wondered if she was going to hit her.

'Marie, what have you been *doing*? Why did you go with Jean-Pierre?'

'He said – that if I helped him to convince Didier we were trying to help him – ' Her words tumbled out in a rush.

'How?'

'We said we'd get him out – from the hospital. I think he believed us. He's so – strange.'

'In exchange for?' Mireille's voice was ice.

'He should tell us what he knew.'

'And then – you'd have ammunition for blackmail. Both of you. Am I right?'

'Yes. But he told us nothing. Nothing in the end.'

'You must go straight to the police.'

'No,' said Marie. 'I can't.'

They continued to argue but Marie was adamant. Finally, sick at heart and determined to tackle her sister again in the morning, Mireille lay on her bed, trying unsuccessfully to rest. Half an hour later she rose and went back to Marie.

'Did you just do it for the money you might get?'

Suddenly Marie knew she should tell her sister everything, but was far too terrified to go any further – to confide any more.

'Yes.'

'Why?'

'Because we need it.'

Mireille went back to bed, unable to understand but too horrified to talk any further. Meanwhile, Marie closed her eyes, knowing that she should tell her but feeling too exhausted, too weak to go into it all.

The grounds of the château rambled away into hilly, pine-wooded countryside. The lawns were neatly mowed at front and back and a flight of wide steps led up to a glass-fronted entrance. As he rang the bell, Marius noticed how well kept everything was from the immaculate tiled floor in the entrance hall to the deep pile carpet that led away down the corridor into its interior. But there had been an emptiness to the place since Alain had lived here along with his pictures and his books and his music. It was as if he had wrapped himself in a cocoon, and although the château and its grounds were regularly cleaned and maintained, there was an atmosphere of aridity. Even now, as Alain walked towards Marius with a welcoming

135

smile, dressed in a rather formal tweed suit and bow tie, he looked as if he was somehow preserved in a still, shut away world of his own.

'Marius. Welcome.'

'Thank you for inviting me.'

'Georges has laid out a cold lunch in the garden. I hope it's going to be adequate.'

'I'm sure it will be.'

'Would you like to wash?'

'Thank you.'

As he washed his hands in the marble basin, Marius looked out over the lawn. The table was laid with a snow white linen cloth and Georges was fussing over the wine. The lawn was trim and green, despite the heat, and further down Marius could see a line of sprinklers playing on the grass. There was a pair of statues on the gravel – winged horsemen – and a dazzling fountain played, its spume sparkling against the cloudless sky. Marius had always loved the fountain. Its centre-piece was a huge swan and the water dropped in an arc from its throat and under its wings with a rhythmic sound.

When he came down, Alain was already seated at the table, a sun hat cocked over his eyes and a handkerchief protecting the back of his neck. He no longer looked vulnerable, but had returned to his more familiar distinguished air of quiet, authoritative confidence. Georges gave Marius a St Raphael and then disappeared back into the house.

'Well, Marius. Are you going to stay?'

'For a while.'

'And you're going to stay at home with your mother, attend the inquest on your father, battle with Estelle and keep your head low?'

'She's not such a battle now.'

'But aren't you tempted?'

For a moment Marius wondered what the hell Alain meant. Then he realised he was not talking about Estelle.

'You mean to investigate on my own? How can I? It's not my case.'

'Marius, I was going to mention this to you the other night. But – somehow I felt it would be wrong to drag up conjecture. Conjecture of my own.'

'Wrong?'

'Ill-advised. But after this latest atrocity . . .' Alain paused and looked abstractedly at the fountain. Then he turned back to Marius. 'I have a great deal of time in which to think. But have you ever considered the possiblity that Suzanne Rodiet wasn't necessarily shot for interfering – for trying to protect those young people? That she wasn't necessarily shot by the Germans?'

Marius looked at Alain warily. 'You say this is all conjecture?'

'Purely. It's just another possiblity. But I see no reason why she should have risked her own life by intervening and trying to save those young men's lives, though she did know the mother of one of them. Why was she present anyway? Why should she be there?'

'Tip-off? Easy enough.'

'Possibly. But why should Suzanne get a tip-off and arrive just in the nick of time to start protesting? Maybe it's something someone thought she should have done. That it explained why she was there – why she died.'

Marius was silent, trying to analyse the implications of what Alain was suggesting.

'What are you trying to say, Alain?'

'I always suspected Suzanne of collaboration. She was an enigma. She seemed to have this – almost false identity. It seemed so shallow – as if she had made it up.'

'Suzanne Rodiet always appeared as one of the main victims of the tribunal,' said Marius.

'I think it was she who gave away the young people in the first place.' Alain spoke very softly. 'She, too, was friendly with Commandant Kummel.'

'Why was nothing said at the time?' demanded Marius.

'Very few people knew, and those who did believed she was seeing Kummel to take information back to the Resistance.'

'Like my father?'

'I've always suspected that, unlike Henri, Suzanne Rodiet could have been some kind of double agent. I know it sounds melodramatic. Absurd.'

Marius looked at Alain intently. He was confident, choosing his words carefully. And none of it sounded absurd at all – even if it was conjecture.

'What's your evidence?' Marius wanted something much more definite.

'There were tip-offs about some of the Maquis raids – I'm sure they came from Suzanne.' But Alain's voice had lost its crispness and he seemed deflated.

'But if you suspected all this,' Marius said slowly, 'why the hell didn't you say anything about it when my father was alive?'

'We discussed her many times, but your father was always adamant that I was wrong.'

'Why?' asked Marius curiously.

'He said he knew she was innocent – but he never gave any hard facts.'

'But it was official, wasn't it? That the Germans shot her?' persisted Marius.

'That was what we were told. But there was nothing official. Only rumours. Like there were rumours about Henri.'

Marius stared at him with sudden amazement. 'Are we suggesting that *Gabriel* killed my father – and Jean-Pierre? Just to protect his mother – assuming of course that Jean-Pierre knew as well?' Marius laughed. 'He hated her.'

'I'm not making any such suggestion.'

They sat silently, sipping their drinks, suddenly unable to communicate.

'If there was a double agent in the Maquis – that person could equally well have been my father,' Marius said at last.

'Or dozens of other people,' replied Alain drily. 'And Henri could never have been a Nazi agent. I knew him – he was a man of total integrity. You can rule out any doubts about him.'

'Did your sisters know Suzanne Rodiet?'

'Slightly.'

'Have you ever discussed your theories – your conjectures – with them?'

'There wasn't much opportunity. As you know, we fell out after the war.' His voice was sour.

Marius nodded. 'But I can talk to your sisters – '

'It may be difficult. They are not easy people. And there is nothing I can do to help you.'

'No.'

'So what *are* you going to do?' Alain's voice was impatient.

'I'm going to take you seriously,' Marius replied softly. 'I'm going to try and find out 'what I can about Suzanne Rodiet.'

'The trail may have gone very cold.'

'I realise that.'

'I'll give Georges a call now,' said Alain suddenly, after a short silence. 'We should start our lunch.'

'Alain, I'm sorry to be so single-minded but are you really certain – did it never enter your head that my father *could* be this double agent?'

'No,' replied Alain. 'He would have been quite incapable of ever doing that. He was genuinely pumping Kummel for the Movement and reporting back to Solange. I'm sure of it. Georges!' He rang the bell.

As Georges emerged from the house, bearing a tray of food, Marius felt a curiously heady mixture of soaring anticipation and raw fear. But at least he had something to do.

Although Jean-Pierre's body had been removed, there were still police around the Claude cottage at four in the afternoon. Marius skirted the activity and headed for the other side of the lavender field. He had drunk a considerable amount of good claret at lunchtime, rounded off by several armagnacs. His head swam as he walked and once he reached the other side of the field, he flopped down, staring up at the rocky foothills and the Alps beyond.

Marius dozed, and as he drifted into sleep the image of the mountains stayed in his mind. He saw a mountain path, then in the hot afternoon sun he saw his father and Jean-Pierre, blindfolded, manacled together, ascending the steeply rising ground, walking slowly, sometimes stumbling. Behind them came a priest, but when Marius could see more clearly he realised the priest was Gabriel Rodiet. Behind him walked a motley procession, all with candles, despite the clarity of the light. His mother and Mariola Claude walked hand in hand followed by Lebatre, on his own and carrying a chalice. Red wine splashed over the top and dribbled down its silver sides, staining the rocks a dull crimson. The Leger sisters walked side by side, followed by André and Annette Valier in single file. Then came Isobelle Rodiet, strangely holding the hand of

Natasha. Then, lastly, some considerable distance behind them, was Alain. His head was thrown back and his hands were clasped behind him. They walked on and on, climbing towards the summit. And there, on the summit, was Estelle, but then she became someone else – a dark cloak of a woman, faceless and without shape. Marius knew that this was Suzanne Rodiet. She looked down and pointed at his father and Jean-Pierre, and as she did so they withered and died until they became two gnarled olive trees. The others gathered around the trees and began to pick their crop of olives. Alain produced a bottle of claret. The picnic began.

Marius awoke, with a dry mouth and a blinding headache. Monique swam into his thoughts, overriding the dream images. Suddenly he knew that he never wanted to come back to Letoric again, that he would marry Monique and maybe they would have children – and maybe live happily ever after in Lyon. His resolution had already dissolved, drifted into confusion during the night. Marius closed his eyes miserably against his indecision and then opened them again. There was a heat haze over the lavender field and for a fraction of a second he thought he saw Jean-Pierre striding through it, 'whacking thighed and piping hot'. His mind searched for the source of the quotation but it didn't come. Instead Jean-Pierre strode on until he became like a living Seurat – a mass of dots, transfusing in colour. Then he wasn't there.

Marius lay on his face, pressing it on to the warm earth, smelling the lavender-scented mould – that Jean-Pierre would soon become. That his father would become. He began to sob but no tears came. A light wind blew over the field, mercifully caressing his hair; suddenly it dropped and immediately the dead heat came back. Marius sat up. He knew of only one thing he could do: to find out who killed them, to find out who sat at the tribunal, to find out who had betrayed the Maquis to the Germans, the Germans to the Maquis.

He got up quickly, putting in abeyance his decision over Letoric and with that his mother, Estelle, Monique, the future – the whole damned clutter of decision-making. He would attempt to block it all out by taking up the investigation professionally.

As Marius walked slowly back to Letoric, his head cleared. He had always respected Alain – for his intelligence and his discernment. But now that he was sober, Alain's theory became more and more unsatisfying. A long-dead woman, the vague idea of a double agent based on incidents and interventions in the Maquis that could have been caused by anyone or anything, by coincidence, by chance, by . . . Then he realised he had never talked deeply with Alain Leger. And now he was propounding theories, reaching out to him, forming a friendship based on present sympathy and past mysteries. Indecision began to erode his new sense of resolution. Without hard evidence, Marius knew that any private investigation of his own would be almost impossible. For a moment he was tempted to ring Gabriel and share with him what Alain had told him, but some instinct prevented him – at least for the moment.

That night André and Annette Valier dined together at Le Clozel at a far table on the terrace by the river. The atmosphere between them was charged with recrimination and Annette could hardly wait for the aperitifs before attacking.

'It's all over the town.' She sat back in her chair and swallowed a large portion of her gin and tonic.

'I wouldn't have agreed to dine with you here if I'd known you were going to chastise me.'

'Oh for God's sake . . .' She drank more gin in contempt. He hadn't used his little boy lost expression in years. It nauseated her. All day she had been bubbling with anger, finding the anger a catharsis. Annette no longer cared what she said to him and despite his withdrawal, she no longer cared what happened. She had spent too long being careful. The news had filtered through to her via André's secretary – a confidante of hers rather than his. Originally she had been suspicious of Janine's friendliness, her desire to 'tell' on her husband. Then, some months ago, Annette had realised that Janine seemed to have a fixed dislike of André; despite this, she stayed working for him – and running him down to Annette. At first she had coldly discouraged Janine's confidences, but since André had become more distant, she had begun to encourage them. One thing she was sure about – Janine was not André's mistress.

141

Maybe she would like to be but she wasn't, for Janine was domineering, managing, unflattering – all the things André most hated in a woman.

'Look.' He changed from little boy lost to hard-edged journalist in seconds. Annette grinned. He was going to talk to her like a grown-up, as if they were both grown-ups who knew the wicked ways of the world – who shared them. 'We're an investigative newspaper; we've got that reputation to uphold. So I tried with Leger. And Claude. It didn't work.'

'You blew it.'

'No. I took a risk and it didn't pay off. And as for being all over the town – ' He paused suspiciously. 'You haven't been speaking to Janine, have you?'

'Why should I? She's the soul of discretion.'

'I sometimes wonder.'

'Then don't. She gives me messages about you. About when you're coming home – which is always late.'

'Then it's that bitch – that little slut Estelle.'

'Perhaps. But I heard it all *here*. The waiters knew. I've never felt so humiliated.'

'Oh come on – '

'But they do, André. Don't be a damn fool.' She drank some more of the gin and began to feel heady with power and decision. Annette rarely drank and even more rarely felt confident; the combination was almost euphoric. At the same time she was conscious that Charles, the head waiter, was looking at her and André with undisguised curiosity. She saw him nudge another waiter and she leant forward and whispered to André: 'You've behaved despicably.'

'Look – '

'Persecuted old ladies. Tried to exploit them.'

'You just don't know what you're talking about.' There was a calculated sneer in his voice and suddenly Annette was afraid. André was recovering. He looked around him, leaning back, truculently stretching and grinning.

'Of course I know what I'm talking about. You're nothing more than a gutter journalist.'

That seemed to sting him immediately. 'If you knew anything about – '

'Don't keep saying that. It's so damned arrogant. You

142

exploited three women in the most calculated way: Marie Leger in her hatred, Mariola Claude in her grief – and Estelle in her greed. It was easy, wasn't it? But most editors worth anything wouldn't have touched it. And don't tell me I don't know what I'm talking about.'

'So you disapprove. What of it?'

Again the fear returned to her; she was doing immense damage. She must stop. But Annette knew she couldn't.

'André, don't you care what you do?'

'You sound like a petulant child.'

'Why are you so cruel?'

'I'm trying to find out the truth.'

'Why?'

'I care about Henri Larche.'

'That's the first I've ever heard of it. You care more about the circulation of the newspaper.'

'The police have got nowhere.'

'They'll get somewhere soon. Particularly after what happened today.'

'I doubt it.'

'Why?'

'Whoever killed the two men is clever. And they'll stay clever. There's too much at stake, I'm sure. Larche wasn't killed just for revenge. Neither was Claude. They knew something. That's why I had those women in. I thought I could pump them. And I'll tell you something else – '

'Well?'

'Something personal. Something between us. Something I resent.'

'What are you trying to say, André?'

'We've drifted apart.'

'Madame.' Charles had come up without either of them noticing him. He stood there, head bowed in the gathering darkness, somehow a rebuke to both of them. Perhaps he's frightened too, thought Annette. Maybe he thinks we're breaking up – that the restaurant will suffer.

'We don't want to order yet,' said André. 'Let's have some more drinks. Madame will have a gin and tonic and I'll have a Pernod.'

'Very well, monsieur.' He withdrew and she felt a rush of

compassion for him. He'd been at Le Clozel for many years. He didn't like change, and change was in the air. She knew it as she looked across at André. For the first time in months there was a frankness in his eyes. Was there the same in hers? An air of finality overtook her, and the creeping sense of loss churned in her stomach. Please, André, no. Let's get up. Go. Run. Never talk any more.

'Is there someone else?'

He frowned slightly. 'No.'

'Do you promise me?'

'You have my word on it.'

And she knew she had. But somehow it didn't make it any better.

'Then why?'

'I could ask you that too.'

'Is it because of the baby?'

'No.'

'Then *what*?'

'It's something. Chemistry.'

For the first time in ages they were talking honestly. But she wished to God they weren't.

'André . . .'

'Yes?'

'Can't we try?'

'With your contempt?'

'No. That's only – related to one issue.'

'Mm.'

'Don't you believe me?'

'Here comes Charles.'

He was like an old bird, pecking at them. She noticed that his hand shook slightly as he put the glass in front of her.

'Madame.'

'Thank you.'

Curiously his hand was quite steady as he put André's glass down.

'Thank you, Charles.' André's voice was dismissive. 'We'll call you in a few minutes for the menu.'

'Very well, Monsieur Valier.'

He walked away, his stoop pronounced.

144

'Well, Annette?' He lifted his drink to her. 'What shall we do?'

The words came into her mouth before she could stop them. 'Do you want to separate?'

'Yes.'

'God – André.'

'Well?'

'I didn't think – '

'But I think we *should*.' He was very emphatic. 'Just for a while. Until things sort themselves out.'

'How will they?'

'Just give me some thinking time. And yourself.'

'There *is* someone else.'

'No.'

'Please don't.'

'Then what?' He sounded slightly impatient, as if she was interfering with a prearranged plan. Prearranged? Could it be? Was this what he had been leading up to?

'You stay at the house. I couldn't bear it on my own.'

'Then where . . .'

'Here.' She looked at the river. 'I want to stay here.'

'Will you have some lemon tea, Mireille?'

'I'd rather have a drink.'

'Then have one.'

'Good gracious, Marie, no lectures for once?'

They were sitting in the dim and cluttered formal sitting-room as a protection against the heat that still smouldered in the early evening.

'No.'

'Will you have one?'

'No. I really do prefer tea.'

Mireille got up, poured herself a Scotch and then returned to her chair.

'Listen – you are withholding evidence. Someone out there has killed twice. They may kill again. You *have* to tell the police everything. Now.'

Marie turned away from her. 'I could be arrested. Charged.'

'They can't charge you for something you might have done.'

145

Mireille went over and picked up the portable phone. She placed it in her sister's lap. Then she went to the phone book and looked up the number. 'Phone Rodiet,' she said. 'Shall I dial?'

Slowly Marie nodded. Suddenly she made up her mind. She was going to tell him everything. She looked at her sister, holding the receiver like some kind of weapon. Mireille was going to get a shock, she thought. A devastating shock.

11

Marius spent the afternoon talking to his mother, having dismissed Estelle with difficulty. Eventually she had gone, mouthing noises of discontent.

'Mother, Alain is going to restore Letoric.'

'What?' She turned over and looked up at him warily. 'Why?'

'It'll be a joint enterprise, but he's providing the funding. It'll grow again, Mother – the lawns, the drive, the fountains. Isn't it wonderful?'

It was even more wonderful that she was so suddenly rational. She sat up in bed, eyeing him curiously and intelligently. But when she spoke she sounded like a child.

'What about me?'

'You'll live here.'

'With it all new?'

'Yes.'

'What about the builders?'

Marius smiled. 'I expect they can work round you.'

'Now – ' She started to turn.

'Just one other thing.'

'Well?' Amazingly she was still rational – the longest in days. For an appalling second Marius wondered if it was genuine – if she was really taking in what he was saying or if it was just superficial, another form of her dementia.

'Well?' She emphasised a little more brusquely and Marius hurried not to miss the opportunity.

'Did you know Suzanne Rodiet?'

'Her?' His mother's tone was disdainful.

'Yes. Her.'

'Awful woman. She was a hard bitch.'

'In what way?'

'Your father and I disliked her – she was vile to her quiet little husband.'

'But she was a heroine.'

'That's what they say.'

'Wasn't she?'

'I want to have my siesta.' The smell of lavender blew into the room and the curtain swung in the breeze.

'Give me a few more minutes, Mother.'

'Why?' She turned a staring, beady eye towards him.

'I'm trying to find out who killed Father.'

'Killed him? He's not dead. How dare you say your father's dead?'

'Stop acting!' he yelled and sat back and waited for Estelle to come running in. That was it – he'd lost control. But she didn't come – and his mother was still staring at him.

'Who's acting?'

'You are.' But his voice was unsteady.

She blinked up at him, her blurred features creased into sulky misunderstanding. 'I don't know *what* you're talking about. It's a lot of rubbish,' she said truculently.

But Marius shook his head and plunged on relentlessly. 'You must have summed up Suzanne. You probably knew her very well. And I want to know what you thought of her.'

'I've just told you.'

'Is that all?'

'She took the German army on – and got shot for her pains. That's what they say.' Her voice had gone sing-song again.

'Yes, that's what everyone thinks,' said Marius grimly. 'The point is – is it true?'

Marius' voice was sharper now. He was somehow convinced that she was acting, that for some reason she was hiding behind a false screen of dementia. Then Marius mentally shook himself – he was being absurd. His mother had had a stroke and dementia had resulted, particularly misconceptions of time and place.

'Mother, please – *please* try and concentrate.' He felt as if his frustration would boil over at any minute.

'Estelle!'

'*Please*, Mother.'

'Estelle!'

148

'Yes, madame?'

Marius turned abruptly as she came into the room in a tight-fitting housecoat.

'I'm late for my pills.'

'But you were with monsieur. I didn't like to – '

Marius rose, defeated. 'I'll go.'

'Monsieur . . .'

'Yes.'

'Were you – questioning your mother?' She was hesitant.

'It's no business of yours.'

'That's true, monsieur.'

'Then don't ask.'

'It's just that I don't want to get you into trouble.'

'And how would you do that?' he asked, his attempted sarcasm coming out more bluntly than he had intended.

'I'm being interviewed tomorrow by Inspector Lebatre. I know he was talking to your mother too.'

'So what?' said Marius childishly. He wanted to be a little boy again and stick two fingers up to her arse. Come to think of it, it wouldn't be a bad thing to do now. He'd suddenly noticed that she had quite a nice arse. Strange – only a short while ago he had been revolted by her.

'I thought the Inspector would be angry. He's already angry because Gabriel Rodiet is on the case.'

'On the case? That phrase sounds like a B movie.'

'Monsieur, I am only trying – '

'Listen, Estelle. Rodiet is Lebatre's boss and can question who he likes. And no one can stop me talking to my mother.'

'Yes, monsieur.'

'And Mother – '

'Estelle, my pills. They're *late*.'

'Stop acting.'

'Monsieur – ' Estelle was reproving.

'If you know something about Suzanne Rodiet you must tell me,' he continued. '*And* Lebatre.' He turned to Estelle. 'And if you're trying to get her to hold anything back – don't. Don't collude with my mother. Don't collude with anyone. And that's official. I want the truth.'

*

149

Marius had slept in his father's study for a while and Suzanne Rodiet had danced mockingly through his dreams. He woke, his mouth dry and his head muzzy. Grabbing a bottle of Mâcon and a glass, he fled to the overgrown terrace. It was nine and the sun was beginning to set. Uncorking the bottle and looking down he saw Estelle gazing up at him.

'Monsieur?'

'Well?'

'I've left your dinner on the table.'

'Listen, Estelle. I wouldn't wish to have a paid spy in the house.'

'Me?'

'Yes. For half the town. The whole town probably. And of course, for Lebatre. Maybe even Valier.'

'I could go,' she said indignantly. 'I could leave tonight.'

'You could. But then I'm paying you quite well. Am I not?'

'I am well pleased, monsieur.'

'So bear my observation in mind.'

'Yes, monsieur.' She looked down. Suddenly Marius knew what it was about her that made him so uneasy. He wanted to go to bed with her.

He stood on the terrace, unable to come to terms with this new and unwelcome sensation. Estelle suddenly represented the same kind of sensuality as Jean-Pierre. He wanted her all right, rolling and thrashing over one of the mothball-scented counterpanes in the guest room. Getting into each other and the sweat running down them both. His erection swelling, Marius went to the balcony and looked out, taking a large draught of the Mâcon, trying to recreate her image in the hot air below.

I mustn't, he thought. I mustn't. She's my spy, he thought wildly, my gaoler. I want her like that. I want to grind into her, my wild-cat suppression. I'm going to come now, he thought, anxiety for his new light blue cotton trousers rudely interrupting his sexual fantasy. I'm going to come now and I'll *never* get the stain out. He laughed aloud. Little man syndrome, a colleague had once said. Well, that was him all right. He took another

long draught of wine and felt his erection weaken. Thank God
for alcohol, he mused, the great deflater.

'Marius?'
  'Gabriel.'
  He was taking the call in his father's study.
  'What are you doing?' Gabriel's voice was cold.
  'What's up?'
  'You are doing what we agreed you wouldn't.' Gabriel's voice
was heavy with anger.
  'I'm not with you – '
  'You most certainly are. Leave the questioning of your mother
to us.'
  'So she *is* a spy,' said Marius quietly.
  'What the hell are you talking about?'
  'Estelle.'
  'Yes, well, she told Lebatre when he phoned to fix the time
of her interview tomorrow. And your mother's.'
  'He pays her to inform on me.' Marius' voice was dull and
steady.
  'She does it naturally.'
  'Lebatre is a fool.'
  'He has more brains than we both give him credit for.'
  'I've been talking to my mother. As you yourself originally
suggested. I have that right. Even Estelle mentioned that.'
  Gabriel sighed. 'I am in charge of this investigation, Marius –
not you. You should have kept in touch with me.'
  'What has Estelle told you?'
  'That you were questioning her about my mother.'
  'We need to pool information,' said Marius.
  'Listen, Marius. You could be doing severe damage to this
enquiry. God knows – you're a professional, aren't you? Why
do you persist in – '
  'Gabriel – I want you to come over. Alain has put forward a
theory that – that you should know about.'
  'I should know everything that comes up.'
  'Lebatre?' said Marius provocatively.
  'To hell with him. What do you propose?'
  'Come across now. Let's have a drink.'

151

Gabriel was silent. Then he said reluctantly, 'Estelle . . .'

'We'll talk in the conservatory. Your spy won't be able to overhear us there.' Marius laughed at the irony of the situation.

Where did you leave the car?'

'Right down by the old gates. I walked up.'

Marius picked up a couple of unopened bottles of Mâcon and the corkscrew. He stumbled.

'You're drunk already,' said Gabriel. He was dressed very formally in a light check suit and black shoes.

Marius said nothing as he led the way down the overgrown path to the conservatory.

They settled in the deep gloaming of the conservatory and proceeded to absorb enough alcohol to kill memories of Henri's stiffening body and the gouts of blood that had looked so much like stage paint. Above them, huge dark spiders crawled precariously over the silky network of fly entombed web. The scent of lavender blew in at the door. God – he was beginning to hate it so much. So very much. It seemed to pervade everything. He saw Gabriel's grimace and wondered if he felt the same about that too.

Sitting in two old basket chairs, facing each other, Marius said, 'I saw Alain at lunchtime. He seems to think your mother was friendly with Kummel – that she could have betrayed those young men – and was then shot to silence her.'

Gabriel listened without emotion, and then asked, 'How reliable do you think Leger is?'

'He's an intelligent man of course, but he has no evidence.'

Gabriel shrugged and drank some more wine.

'Haven't you ever wondered about your mother?' prompted Marius.

'No,' said Gabriel. 'My mother's motives have always been very clear to me. I just can't see her in that role at all. She was a cynical, frustrated woman who had made a bad marriage. She found my father weak and irresolute.'

'Did she know any of the young men who were executed?'

'There was one, Marcel Girard. He came to the house a lot. And then there was Pierre Relais. His mother was a friend.'

152

'What about him?'

'I think she was fond of him. But Marcel was more of a favourite. I remember there was a hell of a row about it between my parents and he never came again. Not to my knowledge anyway.' There was a long pause and then Gabriel said, 'I've often thought about her – and tried to conjure up what might have happened. She was the daughter of a farmer. Peasant, really. Thought she'd ensnare my dear naïve father – and she did. For the first few months she must have liked the money, the difference in status. But there can't have been as much of it as she had thought and being a doctor's wife – here in St Esprit – required the sort of work she just couldn't handle. Then she became pregnant and things must have begun to deteriorate. It was all too much for her and she resented me for the additional burden I was.'

'Has anyone ever mentioned to you people she knew – like any high-ranking Germans?' He looked across at Gabriel sharply.

'No.' Gabriel replied positively and returned to the subject of his childhood. He refilled his glass without asking. 'She never knocked me around.' He drank ruminatively. 'Just despised me. I wish she *had* hit me. It would be more positive somehow. Don't you agree? I suppose she despised me like I despise Lebatre. Small man in a small town. No vision.'

'What vision would she have had?' asked Marius mildly.

'That's it. I don't know. She always seemed to be in some vile mood or preoccupied with her own affairs.'

'Any relations?'

'Both my parents were only children – and they perpetuated the solitude and lack of family life by only having me.'

'You don't remember anything of that – day when she died, do you, Gabriel?'

'I was playing the piano and it was about four o'clock in the afternoon. She'd been out all day. Some German officers came to the door but I carried on playing. Then I felt the weight of something taken away.'

'You were relieved?'

'Yes, I can honestly say that I was.'

'And your father?'

'Well – he was a very spiritual man. And the German officers

153

presumably took the official line with him. He was very proud of her.'

'Did he grieve?'

'No. We became closer immediately. He cried at the funeral.'

'Conventionally.'

'I felt his emotion.'

'So?'

'He loved her. After his fashion. He spoke her name on his deathbed.'

'With affection?'

'With reverence. She was a strong woman.' Gabriel belched. His voice was thickening.

'Did he never mention the incident?'

'Father? He died a few years after the end of the war but he always revered her as a heroine. A kind of depersonalised legend.'

'No doubts?'

'None that he ever voiced.'

'And you?'

'I know she did it – that she somehow intervened. But I could never understand why.'

'Girard?'

'To save a callow youth who maybe she'd slept with? To stand between him and the executioner's bullet? That *is* myth.'

'She could well have made the one noble sacrifice of her life.'

'Just not Mother's style.'

'Gabriel – '

'I mean it.'

'So it's possible that she was something else?'

'A double agent?' He laughed. 'She didn't have the – subtlety. I couldn't accept any of that. I'm sure the situation is quite straightforward and it happened as the German officers told it – as we all know it. Alain Leger must have a fanciful imagination.'

'What are we going to do, then?'

'What about?'

'Sharing information.'

'All right then, Marius, I'll turn a blind eye to your enquiry as long as you keep me *fully* informed.'

'But will you?' demanded Marius. 'We're both drunk now.

Will you be saying that in the cold light of day? Or will you change your mind like you did before?'

Gabriel closed his eyes and shivered slightly. 'It almost *is* the cold light of day.'

'Well?'

'You have my word. But keep out of Lebatre's way for God's sake or you'll drop me in the shit.'

'I will, and now I've shared with you, what have you got to share with me?'

'Regrettably, very little. Lebatre's getting nowhere.'

'So you have nothing that could help me?'

Gabriel shook his head. 'If anything does come up, I'll let you know at once.'

Marius opened another bottle. As he did so, he glanced covertly at Gabriel. It was impossible to read anything from his expression, yet Marius had a strong instinct that he was holding out on him.

They went on drinking and talking until the dawn brought smudged light to the lichen-smeared windows of the conservatory. The conversation rambled, leaving the case, muzzily ranging over other topics – the Maquis, St Esprit, the contempt Gabriel had for Lebatre, the offer from Alain to restore Letoric – and on into half-sleep. At six, Marius rose stiffly, went into the house and made coffee. They sat on a broken stone balustrade, watching the mist hang in swathes over the moss-clad cherubim that stared up at the tiny fragments of light blue sky.

'So what has the night resolved?' asked Gabriel, sipping his coffee.

'An understanding between us – that I will hold you to,' said Marius.

Gabriel smiled. 'I'll honour that understanding.'

'Of course,' said Marius. 'That's an essential part of our agreement.'

'Can I have some advance ideas of your itinerary?'

'I thought I'd go and see Mariola – and the Leger sisters – and the Valiers.'

'Today?'

'Yes.'

'You're going to be busy.' Gabriel sipped more of the good coffee. 'And do you have – a central line to your questioning?'

'If I can find out who was the contact with Kummel – your mother or my father – I shall be getting somewhere. But you do realise, Gabriel, I might discover something that could cause you embarrassment?'

'I know that.'

'And is Lebatre on the same trail?'

'Probably. But he's following up information about the six – and their relatives.'

'I realise I could be missing something there.'

'I don't know. You must see how you get on today. And Marius – '

'Yes?'

'Remember I know nothing about this. If you run into conflict with Lebatre I'll jump on you.'

'Obviously,' said Marius drily.

'And if you get in to see Mariola you'll be very lucky,' added Gabriel sharply.

'Gabriel . . .'

'Yes?'

'Could I ever get in to see Kummel himself?'

'Not you.'

'But – could you?'

'I might,' he replied.

'Seriously?'

'Yes,' said Gabriel. 'Seriously.'

There was a long silence. Then Marius said, 'One more thing . . .'

'Yes?'

'When will they release my father for burial?'

'I'm hoping they'll do so the day after tomorrow.'

'I want to bury him – just as soon as I can.'

'You can ring the undertaker – make arrangements.'

'Thank you. Somehow once he's buried, I'll feel at the beginning of something again.'

12

'Estelle.'

'Yes, monsieur?'

He felt feverish – half hangover, half acute fatigue. The lust had been increased by the alcohol, by the long hours of talking with Gabriel. All he wanted was her long sinewy body; he had to have her. Now.

'I – want to talk to you.'

'I'm here.' She gave him a faintly mocking smile.

'In my father's study.'

'Very well, monsieur.'

She preceded him. She was wearing her housecoat and a pair of down-at-heel slippers. When they arrived, the room with its dusty sunbeams seemed cold and sepulchral yet he was running with sweat and had a dry mouth – so dry he could hardly speak.

'Yes, monsieur?'

'I . . .'

'Monsieur?'

'I'll be out all day. How is my mother this morning?'

'Quite bright.'

'You mean – not drifting so much?'

'Something like that.'

'Do you think she puts it on, exaggerates her dementia?'

'No, monsieur. She is very ill.' Estelle sounded scornful.

'Yes. Well . . .'

'Is there anything else, monsieur?'

'No. I'll be back for dinner.'

*

Mariola watched him walking down the lane like a vanquished foe. He was coming to her to ask forgiveness. She leant heavily on the door in the early morning sunshine, curious rather than hostile. A heavy sleep had made her numb, emotionless.

'Madame Claude.'

'What do you want?'

'I want to talk to you. I swear I didn't kill him.' Marius Larche spoke softly. He was unshaven and wearing jeans and a sweatshirt. He looked younger than his years, she thought, despite the bags under his eyes. She no longer felt the terrible loathing for him – just a deep, inner ache, a mother's mourning that would never go away.

'I don't know who killed my son.'

'I thought you were going round saying it was me.'

'I was upset.'

'So you no longer accuse me?'

'I no longer know what to think.'

'Can I come in?'

'If you must.'

'I only want to ask you a few questions.'

'Let's sit outside.' She bestirred herself, an old raven dressed in black dowdy feathers. Yet even her bearded cheeks had a certain dignity this morning.

Outside it was sheltered from the scorching heat of the rising sun by a large chestnut tree. There was a small back yard with a table and a couple of battered white chairs. Somehow he was sure that she often sat here alone. They overlooked the lavender field which dipped and flounced in a light breeze. Further along there was the rough track. Here I am again, thought Marius, sitting at the scene of the crime.

'Do you want something? A little coffee? Or – '

'No thank you. First – please be assured I meant no harm to Jean-Pierre. I was very fond of him – and even asked Rodiet if they would drop the charges.'

'And would they?'

'I think they had the idea of trying to get him into hospital. To dry him out.'

'I know – Lebatre told me.'

There was no way of telling whether she approved or disapproved.

'I want to know about Suzanne Rodiet.'

'Why?'

'I'm wondering if your son knew anything about her – something that might – just might – have caused his death.'

'She was married to a stick of a man. I know my Philippe was a swine, but at least he had some red blood flowing in him.'

'Did she have a lover?'

'I can't say.'

'Come on, Mariola. Be straight with me.'

'I don't know whether she had a lover or not. But she'd have been a fool not to take one.'

Marius tried another tack. 'Is there anything that Jean-Pierre knew – anything he knew about anybody that might have caused his death?'

'He knew a lot.'

'What do you mean by that?'

'He was curious,' she said flatly.

'Do you mean he liked to get information on people?'

Mariola was resolutely silent.

'So he could use it against them? Like he did with me?'

She was still silent.

'Come on, Mariola. Do you want to track your son's killer down or not?'

'He wasn't all bad, my boy,' she said defensively.

'I didn't say he was.'

'We were very poor. Philippe had left us like that. It wasn't the boy's fault.'

'No.'

Marius still felt raw from his desire for Estelle – the same desire he had had for Jean-Pierre. Why hadn't he taken her when he could? What instinct made him stand off? Suddenly he felt terribly thirsty.

'Do you have any cold water?'

'Lemonade,' she pronounced firmly and got up.

'Well. Yes. All right.' Marius was concerned about the kind of concoction she would bring back. But when she returned he was pleasantly surprised. It was home-made, long and cool and full of flavour, as if it had lain for some time in a deep cellar. He drank it carefully, savouring each drop. He looked out beyond the lavender field and thought for a moment he could see Jean-Pierre hunched at the wheel of a tractor. Then the shimmering stopped – and there was nothing to be seen except the rustling fields of sunflowers beyond.

'So who else did he gather information on?'

She was silent.

'Anybody he could blackmail?'

Mariola frowned.

'He went to see Didier – with Marie.'

'Who's Didier? And do you – can you mean Marie Leger?'

Her voice quavered. 'Yes. Marie. Marie Leger.'

Marius, determined to be patient, asked again, 'And Didier?'

'He was in the Maquis but they tortured him. He attacked his mother – and they put him away.'

'In prison?'

'In an asylum.'

'Why should Jean-Pierre and Marie Leger visit this Didier?'

'They thought he knew something.'

'Knew what?'

'I don't know – something about your father, maybe.'

'Did they both have blackmail in mind?'

'I don't know.' She began to emit hard dry sobs. 'I don't know.'

'And has Marie Leger spoken to anyone about her visits – and her motives?'

'Her sister made her call him. She told me her sister insisted on it. And that was the first I knew of it.'

'Call who?'

'Rodiet. Commissaire Rodiet.'

Marius was quiet while she continued to give vent to the ugly sobs. Then he said, 'Can I use your phone?'

'You won't get me into trouble – '

'No. But please – stay in the garden. It's a private call.'

'It's in the main room.'

He left her and walked into the cool dinginess of the house. Once in the dark and overcrowded sitting-room, he dialled Gabriel's number and then asked for his extension.

'Rodiet.'

'It's Marius.'

'Well?'

160

'I'm with Mariola.'

'Anything?'

'You said you had nothing to tell me. Didn't you realise how close Marie Leger and Mariola are? That she would tell her that she had you contacted about seeing Didier?'

'Marie Leger phoned me. But I've yet to interview Didier. That's why I didn't tell you. I don't *know* anything yet.'

'Rubbish,' said Marius bleakly. 'Total bollocks. You never had *any* intention of pooling information, did you?'

'Of course I damn well did. It's just that I had nothing – '

'You're a fool,' said Marius, furiously cutting in on him, 'a damned fool. Marie would have told me – '

'You're wrong. I told her not to.' Gabriel's voice was expressionless. 'And I *didn't* know how close to the old woman she was.'

'And you never meant what you said.'

'I'd have told you – when the time was right – '

'No,' yelled Marius. 'I'm on my own now. And to hell with you.'

'Monsieur Valier will see you now.'

'Thank you.'

Marius wished he had shaved – or had had some more of Mariola's lemonade. He felt terrible, headachy and dehydrated. There was also a slow burning anger in him that Gabriel had not kept his side of the bargain. He should have realised he never would.

The office was as bare and stylish as he would have expected. But André Valier did not match his surroundings. There were bags under his eyes and an over-lived expression to his face.

'Isn't Inspector Lebatre in charge of this case?'

'Yes.'

'So what do you think *you're* doing – pulling rank?'

'No. Shall I go?'

'Yes.'

Marius walked back to the door.

'Wait.'

He turned slowly.

'What do you want to know?' André Valier leant back, looking exhausted.

'Some questions about Kummel – and essentially, of course, any clue you might have uncovered as to who he appointed to chair that tribunal.'

'I can't tell you anything about him – anything that's not already been disclosed.' He spoke quickly. 'You can look at the archives if you like. But there's no clue whatsoever about who presided over that court.'

'You think it was my father, don't you?'

'Monsieur Larche, do you feel the killing of your father and Jean-Pierre Claude are connected?' He was leaning forward now and looking more animated.

'Yes.'

'In what way?'

'Well, I believe that my father was killed for the misguided purpose of revenge – and Jean-Pierre because he knew something about the killer.'

'So why have you come to see me?'

'Did you ever try to trace – as the local police are now – the families of the victims of that execution?'

'Once or twice my predecessors tried to dig out stories about them. But there's hardly anyone left. I honestly don't think they're of importance.'

'Maybe what's happening will bring it all to a head,' said Marius softly.

'Then what would the town live off? It's been feasting off its own conscience too long.' There was a pause, then André Valier said: 'Do you think – there are more killings on the way?' He spoke abruptly.

'I don't know. But there's no time left.'

'How do you make that out?'

'Events. Somebody's out of control.' Marius stared round the room, suddenly aware of its arid modernism. He knew he was voicing this thought for the first time, as if André Valier's pugnacious ferreting was crystallising his mind. For the first time since his father's death, Marius' brain was clear, despite his night with Gabriel.

'Somebody near you? Near your family?'

162

'Now you're pumping me,' said Marius. 'I wanted to ask you about Suzanne Rodiet.'

'The lady who intervened. It was Madame Claude who knew her best.'

'I can't get much out of her,' said Marius guilelessly, hoping that he was leading him on a little.

'Neither could I,' said André Valier smoothly. 'But she's a confidante of one of the Leger sisters, isn't she?'

'Which one?' said Marius, hoping to draw him out.

'Marie. She's been good to the old lady. And she's a person one can confide in, don't you think? Single, dumpy, unimaginative.'

'You found this out when you – er – invited them to come to the office?'

'An unsuccessful invitation. But yes.'

'So you think Marie might know a little more than we do about Suzanne Rodiet?'

'I think she might. All I've ever seen in Suzanne is some kind of stereotype.'

'Domineering, impatient, possibly the lover of one of the executed young men. A bully to her doctor husband. Not much time for her son.'

'I can't add anything to that.' André Valier stared at him – and Marius returned the stare. Then they both laughed spontaneously. Strangely, out of an unpromising encounter, a new respect had been born between them.

'I'm sure you can't. No one can. That's the point.'

'You mean she's become something she wasn't?' asked André perceptively.

'I just don't know. But I can't accept her as she was. It's as if there was a set story – a personality concocted about her. But I do have a name that you might know.'

'Who?' He looked uneasy.

'Someone called Didier.'

André's unease left him. 'Yes. I know of him. He's in the secure unit of the psychiatric hospital at Aix.' He paused and then asked a little too innocently, 'Who drew your attention to him?'

'Mariola Claude,' said Marius with a show of frankness. 'That was something she did tell me.'

'Something important possibly. I've already tried to get into

163

the hospital, but there was no way they'd let me. You could use official clout.'

Then how the hell did they get in, wondered Marius. 'Risky when you're not official,' he said shortly.

'Lebatre doesn't know about this?'

'He's been to see you?'

'Not yet. He's still busy tracking down members of the families. Personally I think it's closer to home. Don't you?'

'I couldn't say.'

'Meaning you won't.'

'What do you want in return for Didier?'

'An interview with him. His surname's Gaillard.'

'I don't know if I could swing that.'

'You could try.'

'Rodiet would be livid.'

'It could be a private arrangement.'

'I'll have a go.' Marius got up. 'Thanks.'

'Better than squabbling,' replied André Valier. He also rose to his feet. They shook hands, each experiencing an unexpected spark of liking for the other.

'You are silly.'

The Leger sisters were in the small stone-flagged kitchen, making a simple lunch. The atmosphere was charged with Marie's anxiety.

'They're not going to take action against you. Commissaire Rodiet told you that. And you've made a statement now – '

'But supposing he changes his mind? And they come and take me away?'

'They won't.' Mireille was soothing. 'It's all over.'

Marie Leger listlessly watched the two eggs boiling. She didn't share her sister's confidence and she felt not only great anxiety but a sense of foreboding. Despite her resolution, her statement had not included the full story. 'I'm going out after this,' she muttered.

'Where to?'

'I want to talk to Mariola.'

'I don't think that's a good idea.' Mireille's voice was heavy with disapproval.

164

'She's my friend.'

'She's certainly not. Mariola Claude is a cunning old lady – a wicked old lady.'

'How can you say that – with her son dead?' shouted Marie. 'Don't you have any compassion?'

'Not for her sort,' replied Mireille prissily.

'Then you're a bitch.'

'*What?*'

'A miserable sanctimonious bitch.'

'Have you taken leave of your senses?'

'No. I'm just regaining them.' She grabbed the saucepan of eggs and threw it to the floor. Then, to her sister's fury and amazement, she walked out.

'Your credentials?'

'Here.'

'Thank you.'

The hospital was dramatically imposed on the Aix skyline: an old château, complete with turrets and moat. As he had driven nearer Marius had felt more and more oppressed by its weighty insignificance. Once in the bare and sandy grounds, he drove to reception and was eventually ushered in to the duty doctor. He was young but quietly competent, with a large moustache and steel-rimmed glasses. There was an aura of reasonableness to him that Marius hoped boded well.

'And you want to see Monsieur Gaillard – Didier Gaillard?'

'I am pursuing an investigation. He could be central to my enquiries.'

'We have already had a colleague of yours here – Commissaire Rodiet.'

'Yes. I'm following up his visit with a few further questions.' Marius wondered if he was coming across – and then decided he was.

'You realise Monseiur Gaillard has been here since 1948 – over forty years?'

'Yes. I am aware of that.'

'You do realise he is in the secure wing?'

'Commissaire Rodiet says it is possible to hold a conversation with him,' Marius lied hopefully.

'You would be unlikely to elicit much from him. I'm sure Commissaire Rodiet told you that.'

'He did but I'd still like to try.'

'Very well.' The doctor reached for a key above him and stood up.

Marius leapt to his feet – maybe a bit too quickly, he thought immediately. But it was too late now; anyway, it didn't seem to matter. The young doctor was leading him out of the room and down a flight of stairs. The walls were painted green and blue – a hideous combination. Then they were outside, walking across a volley-ball court that was locked in heat shadow. It was time for the siesta and there was no one around. Their footsteps echoed sharply on the flinty ground.

'Is he violent?' asked Marius, risking a question now they were on the way.

'Not when medicated.'

'And if not?'

'He is violent to himself.'

'Was he always suicidal? Is that why he was admitted in the first place?'

'He tried to kill his mother,' said the doctor flatly.

'Do you know if he was a member of the Resistance?'

'Yes. I believe he was. He is not one of my own patients. I specialise in schizophrenia.' The doctor paused. 'Of course, if you weren't here on official police business, there could be no question of your seeing him without the permission of his doctor.'

'Of course not,' said Marius hastily, and to his relief the doctor started walking again. 'But does he have any visitors?'

'Most of his family are dead now, I believe. Although there's still a brother.'

'Yes. But can you remember *any* recent visitors – not family? It could be very important to my enquiries.'

'Over the last few years there have not been very many visits. But during the recent weeks there have been a few. There was a couple who came, for instance. I believe they had the permission of Didier's brother.'

'Do you know who they were?'

'The visitors. Yes – I took them over there the first time. A Monsieur Claude and Mademoiselle Leger. They had a letter – and we are anxious to encourage visits.'

'Can you describe them?' said Marius sharply.

Rather reluctantly the young doctor complied. There was no doubt at all. His description fitted Jean-Pierre and Marie exactly.

'They came more than once?'

'Yes.'

'They always came together?'

'Yes.'

'And how many times?'

'Twice. Maybe more than twice. Your colleague has, however, asked the same question.'

'I know,' said Marius smoothly. He felt a sudden rush of elation. At least he was getting somewhere. He didn't know where, of course. But at least it was somewhere. It was unfortunate, of course, that Gabriel had been there before him.

'Mireille's gone into the town.' Marie Leger picked up the dirty coffee cups.

'Don't clear away.'

'Wouldn't you like some more?'

'No.'

'A liqueur?'

'Well – '

'I was going to have one myself. Framboise?'

'That would be nice.'

She went into the dark interior and emerged seconds later with two cognac glasses brimming with the liquid.

'That's rather generous.'

'I like to taste it,' she said, subduing all thoughts of her weak digestion.

'And have you seen Didier recently?'

'No.' She was beginning to tremble and some of the liquid slopped over the edge of the glass and ran stickily down her fingers.

'Come on, Marie. I've seen you. It was an accident that I caught sight of you the first time – a very lucky accident.'

'*Seen* me?'

'You've been to visit him with Jean-Pierre – twice. I watched you the second time. You shouldn't have done that.'

'Why?'

'What did you find out?'

'Nothing.'

'Did he tell you about me?'

'Why should he?' Suddenly Marie realised everything. 'It was you who killed Jean-Pierre.'

'Yes.'

'And Henri?'

'That's right.'

'And now you've come for me.'

'That's right – you took the wrong initiative.'

'I was going to the police.'

Marie's visitor laughed. 'You should have been more decisive. I'm in time. Aren't I?'

'Will you stop after this?' She began to shake uncontrollably. Yet she still didn't believe that it was happening.

There was no reply.

The room was bare but painted in soft pastel colours. There was a bed, wardrobe, table, television set and cassette deck, a couple of shelves of books, mainly to do with natural history, and an easy chair by the window. Marius caught a glimpse of a magnificent view of the mountains through the thick iron bars.

'Didier.'

He didn't look up.

'I have a visitor for you. An Inspector Larche. He wants to ask you a few questions about the war.'

Still he didn't look up.

'I'll leave you with him,' said the young doctor. 'If you want me, ring the bell. Just by the door here.' It was discreet but reassuring. The doctor went, softly closing the door behind him.

'It is good of you to see me, Monsieur Gaillard.'

The man turned to him and Marius saw with a shock that he looked curiously young, as if all emotion and worry-lines had been cleansed from his face for years. He was completely bald and smelt of baby powder. There was something in this combination of baby looks and smell that Marius found quite terrifying.

'I don't mind seeing you.' His voice was institutionalised,

slightly sing-song. On his lap was a collection of Maupassant stories, dog-eared and clearly much read. 'Although I don't know if I can be of any use to you.'

The only other chair was a hard one, wedged in under the table. Marius pulled it out with difficulty and then dragged it over to sit beside Didier.

'I gather some friends of mine visit you.'

'Yes?'

'Jean-Pierre Claude and Marie Leger.'

'But Jean-Pierre is dead.'

'Yes.' Marius felt foolish for assuming he wouldn't know about the murder.

'I heard it on the TV.'

'A great tragedy.'

'He was murdered. Like the old man.'

'That's right.'

'Did you come to talk to me about them?'

How old is he, wondered Marius. He could be any age. His father's age? Suzanne Rodiet's age – if she had lived? Or was he much younger? It was impossible to tell.

'Yes.'

'It's funny them coming. I've been here a long time.'

'Did they ask you questions?'

'Many questions.' He didn't make eye contact with Marius at all. Instead his eyes roved round the room, the little black pupils never still. The flesh on his face was pudgy, pale, with clear spots of red on either cheek. Marius wondered whether Didier ever went out in the sun.

'About the war?'

'Yes.' His voice was bright, obedient.

'Were they surprised by what you said?'

'Oh yes. They didn't know I was here.'

'Where did they think you were?'

'Everyone thinks I'm dead.' He gave a clear bell-like childish laugh. 'But I'm not. I've been here. Hiding.'

'Hiding?'

'I know things.' His voice was gleeful. 'People never thought I knew things. Good old Didier. Stupid old Didier. They wrote me off. They did.'

'But not Jean-Pierre. Not Marie.'

169

'Not them.'

'Will you tell me what you told them?'

'I told them a lot,' said Didier triumphantly.

'Where did you start?'

He paused and his fat fingers went to a bag he was clasping in his lap. 'Would you like a bon-bon?'

'No – you have one.'

'Then – I won't tell you.'

'OK – perhaps I will have a bon-bon.'

'Everyone *has* to have a bon-bon with Didier.'

'OK.'

Marius flinched as the soft fingers touched his with a piece of confectionery. They were hot and dry, as if Didier had a permanent fever.

'Now tell me.'

'Where shall I start?'

'Where you think you should start.'

'With Suzanne Rodiet.'

'You knew her?'

'Oh yes. I had relations with her,' he said baldly.

What do I believe, wondered Marius. The old-young face was completely expressionless.

'You had sex with her?'

'You're *not* to use that word.'

'Why?'

'Mother said.' Of course, thought Marius. Better leave it alone. Mother fixation. Either that or – appalling thought – Didier was enjoying lying. Enjoying sending him up.

'So you had relations with Suzanne Rodiet?'

'Oh yes.'

'When?'

'In the war. I was in the Resistance.' Well, I can corroborate that with Alain, thought Marius. Aloud he said:

'I gather she was a domineering woman?'

'She was scared,' said Didier surprisingly.

'What of?'

'What he was doing.'

'Who?'

'Kummel – and her husband.'

170

Marius felt as if someone had suddenly punched him in the stomach.

'What were they doing?'

'Well, Kummel liked boys. And the Nazis didn't allow that, did they?'

'You mean he was a homosexual?'

'Yes. He liked boys. It never came out in his trial, did it?' He giggled slightly.

'And how did he get them?'

'Good old Rodiet. That's what Rodiet was doing. Finding the boys. Didier knows. I was in the Resistance.'

'So – '

'Rodiet found him boys. He met them in a hotel.' He spluttered with laughter and then his face fell. 'Suzanne – I liked her. She was strong. But things happened – things went wrong. Rodiet told me to help him – and I had to. I had to.'

'What did you have to do?' asked Marius gently.

'I had to do it – do things with men.' He smiled.

'Were there other Nazis involved?' asked Marius suddenly.

Didier gave him a crafty look. 'I don't want to tell you.'

'Why?'

'It's a secret. Didier's secret.'

'Did you tell Jean-Pierre? Marie Leger?'

Didier shifted uncomfortably. He nodded.

'Which?'

'Jean-Pierre. He came on his own once. That was nice.'

'And you told him?'

'Yes.'

'Did you tell Commissaire Rodiet?'

'Her son. He came to see me.'

'Did you *tell* him?'

'No.'

'Will you tell me?'

'I might. Have another bon-bon?'

'Thanks.' Again the marshmallow fingers. Marius began to sweat. The room didn't seem to have any cooling system. And there was a strange smell now – a kind of medicated sweat. 'So – the young men. *They* never shot a German officer.'

'They did.'

'Why?'

171

'It was like rape. They killed him because they didn't want to do it any more. Didier didn't want to do it any more.'

'Then the tribunal – '

'Yes.'

'Were *you* there?'

'I was at the court.'

Marius could hardly breathe. 'Who presided over it?' he managed to get out. But Didier was still anxious to tease.

'Didier knows.'

'You told Jean-Pierre?'

'Yes.'

'Marie Leger?'

'She hasn't been,' he said evasively. 'Did she send you?'

'No.' Desperately Marius tried to be patient. 'Didier . . .'

'Mm?'

'The person who presided over the court . . .'

'Yes?'

'Who? Who was it?'

'It had to look right. They wanted someone respectable.'

'Who?' Marius was tense, desperately straining his ears for Didier's reply.

'It's a secret.'

'You've been here a long time,' said Marius, determined to subdue his frustration, to be patient.

'A very long time. You see – I tried to kill my mother.'

'Why?'

'She was angry with me.'

'About having to do it with men?'

'Yes.'

'How did she find out?'

'I expect Suzanne told her.' His voice was careless, matter of fact.

'It wasn't your fault.'

'Mother said I was dirty – she didn't want me in the house.'

'And you were put in here?'

'In 1948. I almost came out – on parole. If that bastard hadn't stopped me.'

'What bastard?'

'Gabriel – the police chief. Gabriel Rodiet. The one who came to see me. He keeps me in here.'

172

'Does he?'

'He doesn't want me to come out, ever.' His voice rose petulantly and he got up and walked to the window. 'I watch birds,' he said absently. 'Birds and lizards.'

'Will you tell me your secret?' whispered Marius.

'What will you buy me?'

'What do you want?'

'Bon-bons.'

'Very well.'

'You promise?'

'I promise.'

'I'll tell you then,' said Didier, his face glistening with a pallid sweat. 'I'll tell you my secret.'

'Who was the man in charge of the tribunal?' asked Marius slowly and painfully.

'Dr Rodiet,' said Didier brightly. 'When will you get me my bon-bons?'

13

Annette was discussing next week's menus at Le Clozel when Mireille Leger arrived hesitantly on the terrace. The noise of the cicadas seemed particularly loud tonight and the water reflected a smoky green under the coloured light bulbs that were strung near its surface.

'Mireille. This is a pleasant surprise.' Annette was actually pleased to see her. She needed to fill her time – use up all her time on anything, no matter how trivial it was. André had moved out after all, presumably to the flat over the office, and the house in St Esprit was echoingly empty. She felt no hope for the future. This was the way it was going to be, but for the moment she couldn't face up to it.

'I can't stay long. It was my turn to be in the shop all afternoon and we've been terribly busy.' She looked puffed, out of breath.

'Why don't you sit down? Have a drink.'

'Oh, I couldn't.'

'It's early. We won't have any customers till nine.'

'But – '

'Have something. An aperitif.'

'Oh – all right.' She looked round the empty terrace vaguely. 'Where shall we sit? There are so many tables.' She gave a little laugh. 'What with one thing and another, I can't make decisions any more. Isn't it ridiculous?' She was obviously asking Annette to share the thought and she did, laughing lightly, guiding Mireille to a seat and signalling one of the waiters. When she had ordered two St Raphaels, Annette leant back in a pretence of relaxation – and Mireille did the same.

'I – er – I came about the cushions.'

'Oh yes?'

'I've just had a cheque.'

'From the paper – '

'Yes. I'm not sure I can accept it.'

'Why not?' asked Annette.

'Well – we were no use to your husband. I mean – my sister wasn't.'

'I wouldn't let that worry you,' said Annette firmly.

'But it seems like taking money under false pretences.'

'Not to me.'

Annette looked around her, hoping that Mireille would follow her gaze. She did.

'They'll look lovely here – I gather you fill some of them with herbs.'

'So your husband is – '

'Buying them for me.'

'Well – '

'It's kind, isn't it?' she said with irony.

'Very.'

'Particularly when he's using newspaper money.' The drinks arrived and Annette stretched out an eager arm. *'Santé.'*

'Your health.'

'How quickly can you get them to me?'

'I've got *some* in stock,' she began doubtfully. 'But I'll have to make the rest. Most of them, really.'

'How long?'

'I'm afraid you've taken me by surprise. My order book's at home. I could ring – '

'Can I come back with you and find out?'

'But – '

'It would be so much quicker.' And it would fill up the evening, thought Annette desperately.

'Of course, you're most welcome.'

'It's just that I want to refurbish the place anyway, and if I knew when the cushions might be ready – '

'Goodness – you can't be basing your redesign round my cushions.'

'They're integral,' Annette lied. 'I love the colours.' Well – they certainly weren't bad, anyway. 'Let's have another drink and go.'

175

'I'm afraid I couldn't manage – '

'I'll have a quick one then,' said Annette. She needed it.

Mireille drove slowly and lumpily in the Deux Chevaux which smelt of dried flowers and pot-pourri. She said little, keeping her eyes on the road, as if driving required all her energies. After what seemed like an interminable journey, they arrived at the cottage. It was dark now but there was a light burning in the front room.

'Will you have coffee?' asked Mireille, panting a little. It was stiflingly hot.

'Thanks.'

'I'm afraid my sister may be asleep.'

Annette looked at her watch. It was nine.

'She's been very tired recently.'

'Really?'

'I think it must be all these dreadful things happening.'

'Quite.' Annette got out and stood by the front door while Mireille fumbled with a key.

'It's so *hot*,' she muttered.

'Isn't it?'

At last she managed to get the door open and they walked into the interior. Thank goodness, thought Annette. At least it's cooler in here.

'Now look at that,' said Mireille brusquely.

'What?'

'That silly sister of mine – she's gone and left those windows open.'

'Perhaps she's hot.'

'She'd never leave them *open*.' She crossed hurriedly to the doors, took them in both hands and paused. 'Hallo.'

'What's up?'

'The furniture's been moved.'

Annette looked around her – everything seemed to be orderly enough.

'Looks like someone's moved this chair and then put it back – but not quite right.' Mireille seemed to be thinking aloud and Annette felt a sudden sharpening of her attention. 'Maybe

176

she's on the terrace,' said Mireille brightly. She bustled through and Annette slowly followed.

The blood on the floor of the terrace seemed to lie in great dark lagoons. There were black splashes on the wall of the house, the furniture and the tubs of geraniums. The carnage was incredible. Annette turned away, beginning to vomit, but Mireille simply stared down at what looked like a heap of clothes, carelessly piled up behind a dark spattered table.

In an involuntary movement Mireille pulled off the blood-spattered tablecloth, bringing with it two empty coffee cups. They smashed on the terrace and the noise was appalling. Marie lay underneath the table. Her throat looked as if it had been torn out. Fingerprints, Annette remembered, as Mireille flung the cloth over her sister's body. She's destroying evidence. But we can't have it staring up at us like this. Not with those eyes. She shuddered, trying to prevent herself being sick yet again by swallowing hard. Whoever has done this, she thought wildly, is a savage beast. Henri Larche, Jean-Pierre Claude, now Marie Leger – throats cut like stuck pigs. Henri, yes; Jean-Pierre, perhaps – but poor old Marie . . . Wiping the vomit from her lips with a napkin which she took from a side-table, and fleetingly wondering if she was destroying yet more evidence, Annette tried to take Mireille's arm. But it was rigorously unyielding, as if there was some great force behind it.

'Mireille – '

'Leave me.'

'Come away now.'

'Where? This is my home.'

'Come with me. We'll go away.'

'There are things to be done. Calls to be made. Don't you realise . . .' She turned round to Annette for the first time. 'Don't you realise – this was my sister?'

'Mother?'

She was sitting on the terrace, staring out at the wilderness gardens of the Château Letoric. Estelle was nowhere to be seen.

'Henri?' She started.

'It's Marius.' He was sorry to have punctured her reverie.

177

Now he knew, Marius was anxious to end it all as soon as possible. But he wanted to make sure she was safe.

'Is that Henri's new maid? I could eat a raspberry soufflé. Have we had lunch yet?'

Marius gave up and called sharply for Estelle. She came after a minute or so, a glass of cognac in her hand.

Did she stagger slightly in the dark? Marius dismissed the thought. He no longer felt any desire for her. Every feeling he had was dominated by a painful despair.

'I want you to take her to bed – and lock the door. *All* the doors.'

'Why, monsieur?' she asked humbly.

'My mother is in danger. Please do as I say.'

'All right.'

'I can rely on you?'

'Of course.'

He suddenly knew he could. 'I may have to go out soon. I shan't be long.'

'Monique?'

'Marius.' Her voice seemed a very long way away.

'I think I might be getting somewhere.'

'You've caught someone?'

'Not yet. But I found someone. Someone called Didier who claims he knows who chaired the tribunal. And it wasn't my father. But he's not a reliable witness. So God knows where I get any real evidence.'

'Are you liaising with the local police?'

'There's no point. Rodiet just holds out on me.'

'So what are you going to do?'

'Talk to Alain – he's my only confidant.'

'And then?'

'Then I'll make a decision.'

'Aren't *you* holding out on *me*?'

'I can't tell you what I suspect. Not on the phone. Besides – there's Estelle.'

'The built-in spy?'

'Yes, her ears are attuned to my slightest inflection.'

They laughed together and Marius felt slightly easier. Then

Monique said, 'If the killer murdered your father and Jean-Pierre for what they knew, why didn't they murder this Didier as well?'

'Because Didier happens to be in the secure unit of a psychiatric hospital. Not that it isn't penetrable – as has been proven. However, killing Didier could lead to a very quick exposure. Someone would be bound to have seen them together.'

'I wish you'd come up here. Even for a day.'

'I can't leave now. Something – someone is out of control here. And I'm on the brink of finding out what I need to know. If only I'd acted earlier – while my father was still alive . . .' Marius' voice broke.

'You just can't have that kind of regret.' She paused. 'Do you know who it is?'

'I have a gut feeling. I could be wrong.'

'I love you, Marius.'

'I love you – my darling. The deadline's ticking away.'

'You make it sound like a death sentence.' There was laughter in her voice.

'No,' said Marius. 'Getting away from this house will be like finishing a long sentence.'

'You mean it?'

'Yes, I mean it. I promise I mean it.'

Gabriel. He had never liked him. Never known him. But his beloved father a procurer of boys for Nazi officers? That quiet, long-suffering doctor, much bullied by his tyrannical wife? Or was that only Gabriel's perception of him? Gabriel's fantasy? He had to talk to him. Marius would have liked to talk it all over with Alain first, particularly as his original conjectures were so close to what Didier had confided – or what he had managed to wring out of Didier.

Marius walked out into the garden, skirting the conservatory and beginning to climb a patch of slowly rising ground that gave him a view of Ste Michelle and beyond to the forest and the foothills. It was a clear night with a slight cooling breeze. There were lights on in the ground floor of Ste Michelle – more lights than Alain needs, thought Marius. Was he entertaining? Did he entertain? It must be a rare occurrence for he had become more

179

and more reclusive over the years. It was comforting, though, to see the lights, to know that Alain's reassuring presence was nearby and that they could talk. He was not alone, but with a senile mother and a servant spy he could become very isolated indeed. Marius walked on into the trees that bordered Letoric and Ste Michelle. He stood there, smelling the pines, wondering what he was going to do next. Then he knew; he had to ring Gabriel and go and see him.

It was Isobelle Rodiet who answered.

'Gabriel's not here,' she said. Her voice seemed odd, almost halting.

Marius looked at his watch. It was 10 p.m. 'He's on duty?'

'He wouldn't be, but he was called out. Don't you know?'

'Don't I know what?'

'There's been another of those bestial murders – one of the Leger sisters this time. He's down there now.'

'Oh my God – '

'It's dreadful – and there must be a maniac on the loose,' she said.

'I'll go straight down there,' replied Marius.

The Leger house was surrounded by police cars, an ambulance, a small Citroën that Marius knew to be Lebatre's and Gabriel's large Peugeot. Showing his card to the officer on the door he hurried through the house to the terrace, which seemed to be the main centre of activity. The area gave the impression of a film set with arc lights and men filling the tiny space. He noticed there was a body bag in the centre of the floor.

Lebatre hurried up to him, discreet but determined.

'I am sorry, monsieur – you have no right to be here.'

Marius said nothing, looking towards Gabriel who was standing on the other side of the terrace, talking to a police officer. Blood seemed to be everywhere.

'I have to see Commissaire Rodiet.'

'He is very busy.'

'Gabriel – '

'All right, Marius. I'm coming.' He looked appeasingly at the furious Lebatre. 'I'll see him in the sitting-room.'

Lebatre shrugged. Somewhere in the background Marius could see Mireille Leger. She had her back to the assembled company and was talking to a detective. Annette Valier stood beside her, her arm around Mireille's waist.

'Come on, Marius,' said Gabriel. 'We haven't much time.'

The sitting-room had a quiet, settled look as they went inside and Gabriel closed the door.

'You shouldn't have come,' he said.

'I had no choice. I've been to the hospital.'

Gabriel looked mystified. 'I don't understand – '

'To see Gaillard – Didier Gaillard.'

'He's a most unreliable witness,' said Gabriel quickly.

'Perhaps. He's made an extraordinary claim – that your father not only procured boys for Nazi officers, but also chaired that damn tribunal. Apparently he told Jean-Pierre and Marie all about it too.'

'Look – we can't talk now.' Gabriel was quite composed, not in the least flustered. 'I'm in the middle of this appalling murder enquiry. Marie Leger looks as if she's been savaged by some wild animal. Whoever it is is as mad as Didier. There can be no doubt about it.' He sat down on the edge of an armchair. 'You've come to confront me, Marius, haven't you? And the reason you're confronting me is because you haven't got a shred of evidence. OK – Didier gets visited by the Jean-Pierre/Marie Leger duo and they were clearly up to no good. But as far as we can tell he told them nothing of any use or they'd have taken some sort of action.'

'They're both dead,' said Marius baldly.

'Yes, but they saw him weeks ago and they had plenty of time to take action. He may not have told them anything.'

'But the murderer suspected he had. So you should put a security alert on Didier.'

'I'm not a complete fool, Marius. As you probably know now, I've already been to see him once. I also checked on him again a few minutes ago. And I've sent a couple of men round to keep an eye on your mother. I suppose you'd left that to Estelle.'

'What else could I do?'

Gabriel nodded.

'I'm working in the dark, Gabriel. And you've kept me in the dark, deliberately.'

'I've done what I can. Lebatre will probably put in an official complaint against me. But there are limits. Listen, Marius – I swear to you that Didier is wrong; my father was never a procurer of young boys nor was he a collaborator. He came into very little contact with the Nazis. All he was, was a quiet country doctor. That I swear.'

'Didier says that you have opposed his discharge.' Marius felt a fool directly he had made the statement.

Gabriel sighed. 'His discharge is nothing to do with me; it's up to the doctors. Look, Marius, all I can do is deny Didier's allegations. He – you – can't make a monster out of my father. Or out of me.' He looked calmly, levelly, into Marius' eyes. 'I didn't cut your father's throat, nor Jean-Pierre's nor Marie Leger's. It's true I had the opportunity. And the reason I was locked in such passionate conversation with Jean-Pierre Claude was that I was desperately trying to get out of him what he knew. And he knew something, but wasn't giving anything away. That's all I can say to you, Marius.' He got up and took Marius' arm. 'Please believe me.'

But Marius didn't know what to believe. Had he made a fool of himself? Was he right to confront Gabriel? 'What level of co-operation can I expect now?' he asked.

'What I said before – as much as I can give you.'

'Which wasn't much.'

'It's all I can do,' said Gabriel sharply. 'I'll get back to Lebatre; he'll be wondering what we're cooking up together.'

'You want me off the premises?'

'It would be advisable. I'll ring you with any details I think you should know.'

Marius knew he was now dismissed.

'Monsieur.'

'Yes?' asked Marius abruptly as he hurried to his car. Then he paused. It was Mireille Leger. She was very composed, very lifeless.

'I'd like a word.'

· 182

'I'm deeply sorry about what has happened.' He spoke very softly.

'Do you know who did this?' Her voice was deliberately calm, entirely without expression.

'No.'

'Please don't lie to me. Do you know who killed her?'

'I tell you – I don't know.'

'Have you seen Didier?'

'Yes, but I couldn't trust anything he said. He's mad – not responsible.'

'You know my sister and Jean-Pierre went to see him?'

'Yes.'

'They had blackmail in mind.'

'Perhaps.'

'My sister was an impetuous, foolish woman. But she didn't deserve to be butchered.'

'Yes, it's just a matter of time,' replied Marius.

'Before they kill again?'

'Before they're caught.' He tried to be as reassuring as possible.

'I find it incredible,' she said. 'It could be anyone. Someone I know very well – who all these years has had something to protect.'

'Somebody to protect,' corrected Marius. 'But it could be a complete stranger,' he concluded, taking her arm. It was very cold. 'I think you should go back inside. You shouldn't be wandering about out here.'

'I'm going to Annette Valier's.'

Behind them, the ambulance started up.

'They're taking her away.' Her voice shook for the first time.

'Yes,' said Marius quietly. 'They took my father. I didn't want him to go.'

She nodded. 'You'll all make them pay, won't you?'

Marius drove up to the Château Ste Michelle. It was a very clear night and the cicadas seemed particularly loud. The stars were brilliant, starkly etched in the black velvet of the sky. Marius felt secure as he drove through the open gates and up the well-kept drive. The lawns were as smooth and green as the sprinklers allowed, and there was some new sculpture over by the lacey sparkle of the fountains. He saw that it was a bronze statue of a girl, beautifully executed, staring down at the dashing water.

He brought the car to a standstill with a crunch on the gravel. Slamming the door he walked up the steps and rang the bell. It seemed a very long time before anyone came. Then he heard slow footsteps and Alain opened the door. He was wearing an open-necked shirt and dark trousers. Thank God, thought Marius. Someone I can really talk to at last.

'Marius.'

'Sorry to call so late.'

'It's good to see you.'

'There's been another one.'

Alain closed his eyes. 'Who?'

'Your sister – Marie.'

Alain turned away, looking grey and ill. He staggered and would have collapsed if Marius had not caught hold of him. He helped him back into the cool interior. There was a lingering smell of good food and coffee. Alain leant against him as they stumbled into the sitting room.

'Thank you.' He sat down heavily in the chair as the phone began to ring.

'I'll get it.' Marius hurriedly picked up the receiver. It was Gabriel.

'Marius. I thought you would be with Alain. Have you – '

'I've told him.'

'I'm ringing officially – but now I don't need to speak to him. Do I?'

'No.'

'Lebatre will need to see him.'

'Not tonight.'

'He'll ring tomorrow.'

'Very well.'

'OK Marius, I'll be in touch.'

Marius put down the receiver and went to pour out a cognac. 'Rodiet,' he said.

'Yes. Yes, of course. Do you want to ask me questions?' asked Alain shakily.

'No. I'm not on the case.'

'Of course not. Silly of me – I keep forgetting.'

Marius told him briefly what had happened, beginning with his visit to Didier and ending with Marie Leger's death and his challenge to Gabriel. He spoke eloquently, slowly. To keep talking seemed the best idea. Alain listened, nodding, occasionally clarifying, intently aware of all he was saying. The original shock seemed to be receding. When Marius had finished Alain said quietly:

'As you say, Didier has little credibility to offer as a witness. I visit him sometimes. He was with us in the Maquis. Poor fellow – he's just a shell now, quite unreliable.'

'Yet Jean-Pierre and your sister went to see him.'

'Yes.' Alain was silent. He sipped more cognac. 'And do you still believe that Gabriel killed to protect his beloved father?'

'I don't know what to believe. There was something about Didier – however crazy he is – that was very convincing. Do you want to stop talking now?'

'No,' said Alain, draining his cognac. 'I don't. But neither do I wish to get drunk. I'd like to remain lucid. I don't want to wake up tomorrow morning and grope around, trying to think of the awful thing that happened that I can't remember – and then remember.'

'I know exactly what you mean.'

'Henri – that peasant – Marie. What next? It's unbelievable.'

'Gabriel has agreed to give protection to my mother – and to Didier.'

'That's good. Unless – '

'He is the killer,' Marius finished. 'But how could he come and go at will from a psychiatric unit?'

'If there was only some way to substantiate what Didier says. Will you see him again?'

'I shall try. But . . .' Marius paused uneasily.

'What is it?'

'My mother. I'm almost certain she knows something, and I just have this feeling that some elements at least of her condition she is exaggerating.'

'So – Henri *did* know something – that he was trying to conceal.'

185

'They all did. I'm sure that's what it all boils down to. In the end.'

They talked on, the hours creeping by, but came to no real conclusion.

'Will you come and stay at Letoric?' asked Marius finally.

'No. I'll be fine here.'

'Shock can be very delayed.'

'Yes. But I'd rather face whatever I have to here. Do you understand, Marius?'

'Yes. I understand.'

Alain showed him out and they clasped hands. Then Marius embraced him and again the old man leant on him.

'Now go home to your mother.'

'I shall talk to her tomorrow. And then to Didier.'

'I've no doubt I shall be seeing the police. And I should have rung Mireille. However estranged we are – I should at least have done that. I'm surprised she hasn't rung me.'

'She's with Annette Valier.'

'Very well. And Marius . . .'

'Yes?'

'I could come and visit Didier with you if you like. It might help with the authorities.'

'I'll ring you,' said Marius as he walked out into the cool moonlight. As he got into the car he turned to look at Alain Leger. He was still standing at his front door, staring out. He looked old, defeated, and he stared up at the stars as if seeking solace. Then, slowly, he walked back inside and gently closed the door.

Marius arrived home at dawn to find a police car parked outside the house and a sleepy-looking officer huddled on the front step.

'Would you like some coffee?' Marius asked.

'That would be nice, sir. Are you Monsieur Larche?'

'Yes.'

'Can I have proof of identification, sir?'

Marius showed him his identity card. 'OK?'

'Thank you, Chief Inspector. We have to check everything very carefully at the moment.'

'Of course. I'll make some coffee.'

A few minutes later Marius came back with two cups of scalding black coffee and he and the policeman watched the dawn slowly come up in quiet companionship. Stretched below them, they could see part of St Esprit; a swathe of mist parted to reveal shuttered houses, still poplars lining silent streets and the church tower, indistinct and floating.

'It's amazing, isn't it – he's out there somewhere. Waiting.'

'Why he?'

'It must be a man.'

Marius smiled at the man's sudden vehemence. 'And we don't even know the murderer's out there. They could be miles away.'

'I don't reckon so, sir.' He seemed very sure. 'They feel local, don't they?'

'Do they? How do they feel local?'

'They know people – I mean, there was hardly any sign of a struggle. Monsieur Larche and Monsieur Claude – and now Mademoiselle Leger.'

'It's true they went trustingly to their deaths. But it doesn't necessarily mean they were lured out by someone they knew. I mean – maybe the murderer posed as an official. As a policeman.'

'Maybe you're right, sir.'

'But you don't really think so.'

'I'm putting my bet on the local man.'

'Grudge?'

'Something they were going to bring to a head, sir, that's why I reckon they were all done in.' He paused, realising he was getting carried away and that he was talking about Marius' father. 'I'm sorry . . .'

'No. Don't be. You've made me think.' Marius looked at his watch. It was six. 'Think I'll try for a couple of hours' sleep. When are you going to be relieved?'

'Half an hour or so.'

'OK – thanks for coming.'

'I hope I didn't speak out of turn, sir.'

'No,' Marius reassured him. 'I told you – you've made me think.'

*

It's a small link I need, thought Marius as he lay awake watching the patch of sky turn blue through the small circular window in his bedroom. Just some small, connecting link – a detail. What had his father known? Did Jean-Pierre and Marie know the same thing? If so, why had they all kept so silent?

14

Marius rose at around eight and went straight in to see his mother. To his surprise she was sitting up in a chair by the bed, drinking coffee.

'Where's Estelle?'

'She died.'

'Mother – '

Estelle arrived with another jug of coffee. 'She couldn't sleep – and she keeps asking for coffee.'

'I could do with some coffee,' said Solange plaintively.

'It's here, my darling.'

'I want to talk to her,' began Marius.

'All right. I'll make myself scarce. I've been up with her all night. She's been restless.' Estelle paused. 'She kept rambling on about the war.'

'Yes?' asked Marius impatiently. He felt utterly exhausted.

'She says Kummel wanted boys or something – I couldn't make out what she was on about.'

'Go on,' said Marius, his impatience rising visibly.

'She kept on about protecting your father – that we all had to protect him.'

'From what?'

'That was the odd thing. I thought she meant the rumours. She said, "Henri's going to tell the truth." She kept saying it over and over again – "Henri's going to tell the truth."'

'One day,' chimed in Solange. Once again her voice had a childish sing-song quality.

'What do you mean, Mother?' asked Marius in as authoritative a voice as he dared.

'One day.'

'What do you mean – "Henri's going to tell the truth"?'

'Soon. He'll have to.'

'Shall I go?' asked Estelle.

'No. Stay. The mistake I made before was trying to do this alone. She's fond of you. She'll say more if you're around.'

'Very well.' Her voice trembled a little.

'You ask her.'

'Solange, my pet.' Clasping both of Solange's hands Estelle repeated the question. 'Why will Henri have to tell the truth?'

'He has to be protected. They can't be found out. Not him and Kummel.'

'Kummel?' Marius blurted out and his mother jumped.

'Careful.' Estelle nudged him. 'Don't startle her.' She spoke very slowly and softly. 'Henri and Kummel? Were they friends or something?'

The old woman nodded.

'How close?' asked Marius. He felt sick and a new, intense desolation was spreading inside him.

'He's dead.'

'Kummel?'

She began to weep. 'My Henri's dead.'

'Who killed him?' asked Marius.

'The Boche,' she replied.

'You won't get anything more,' said Estelle. 'The clarity's gone.'

The telephone rang in the sitting-room just as Marius was about to phone Gabriel.

'Yes?'

'Monsieur Larche. This is Mireille Leger. Can I come up and see you?'

'Of course. When?'

'Would now be convenient?'

'I'll be here.'

She rang off and he sat down at the polished table by the window. Sunbeams picked out the dust that had eluded Estelle's careless regime. Marius closed his eyes. Naturally, if this had been a professional investigation, he would have seen him weeks ago. But to see him might have established his

190

father's guilt, and naturally he had refrained. But now it was essential. Somehow he had to get in to see Kummel. Then he thought of Daniel Foreman – the English war crimes specialist in Interpol. He had come across him several times on other cases and they had both attended a conference in Germany, getting to know each other quite well. Marius looked up his number in his address book and dialled.

'Foreman.'

'Daniel. It's Marius Larche. Do you remember me?'

'Of course.' The voice was hugely reassuring – deep and resonant and arrogantly British. Just what he needed. 'I'm terribly sorry about your father.'

'Thank you.'

'And the chain of events that has followed. It's all been very widely reported in the British press. Seems you have a maniac on the loose.'

'I'm not sure about that.'

'You mean whoever did all that was sane?' He sounded incredulous.

'Determined and desperate I would say. Look, Daniel, I'm not in charge of this case.'

'Obviously not.'

'But I am making enquiries.'

'Oh?'

'I have the – co-operation of Commissaire Rodiet here.'

'You mean he's allowing you in?'

'To some extent. I want you to help me.'

'If I can.'

'I believe the answer to all this lies with Wolfgang Kummel.'

'He's in solitary confinement in Lyon.'

'Yes. I want to see him.'

'That could be difficult. Why?'

'Because I believe he knows who killed my father.'

'I see. And Rodiet?'

'You mean – is he seeing him? No – not as far as I know.'

'Does he have an investigating officer?'

'Lebatre. But Rodiet is – what you might call taking an interest.'

'So really I would have to get you in as a private citizen.'

'Yes.'

'Impossible.' Marius' heart sank; there was a grim finality to Foreman's voice. Then he said, 'Wait a minute.'

'Yes?'

'We are allowing Fergus Rigby in there – you know, the biographer. He's doing a book on Nazi war criminals and we've given permission for him to interview Kummel. There's a possibility I could get you in as his research assistant.'

'That would be marvellous.'

'But it would be much simpler if Rodiet or Lebatre went officially. Much more straightforward.'

'Yes. But I have to come clean with you, Daniel. We got to know each other well in Hanover and I believe you trust me and my professional integrity. My objectivity. Do you?'

'Of course.'

'Then I have to say that I have reason to suspect Commissaire Rodiet of being the killer. He has a strong motive which I don't want to go into now.'

'Good God! But if this comes out – I mean if it's discovered that you went in as Rigby's assistant – I'm not involved. You approached Rigby yourself.'

'Of course. But will *he* agree?'

'Without doubt. He's dependent on me and my French colleagues for access. I shall ring him. But Marius . . .'

'Yes?'

'Be careful. Let me know what happens when it's all over – if it ever is all over.'

'Thanks, Daniel.'

'Don't thank me now. He may know nothing. Goodbye.'

'Goodbye.' Marius put the telephone receiver slowly back on to its rest. He looked at his watch and then out of the window. Mireille Leger was walking up the drive. The intense sunlight gave her a dry, wooden look. But as she came nearer, he could see that there was a strange expression on her face – almost of pleasurable anticipation.

'Can I get you anything?'

'No – no, thank you.'

She was sitting on the edge of an armchair, as if her presence was very temporary. The look was still there; it was as if she was looking forward to telling him something – something that was all-absorbing.

'Monsieur Larche – '

'Marius, please.'

'Marius – I believe my sister could have told the police more than she actually did.'

'Then you should tell Lebatre. He's in charge of the investigation.'

'I will. But I'd – I wanted to talk to you first.'

'You're very welcome. But why?'

'I feel I can talk it all through with you. I don't have any hard facts, you see.'

'Who does in this case? Try me out with your theories.'

'My sister was a very foolish woman, but much of her folly arose out of her hatred for our brother, Alain.'

'After what happened about the estate?'

'Well, yes. It preyed on her mind – all the time. She hated to live as we did. She hated him for making us live as we did.'

'And you don't mind?'

'I did. But I rather enjoy earning a living – carving it out, so to speak. Marie was different. She would do anything to have a better standard of living – to revenge herself on our brother. I honestly feel she had got herself into a very disturbed state.'

'The friendship with Jean-Pierre, the visits to Didier?'

'That and her gossips with Mariola. I'm sure they spread all that vile stuff about your father. And there was the farcical agreement to write for Valier.'

'But that was all against my father. Not Alain.'

'I think she felt she was getting at Alain through Henri – by hitting out at Henri she was hurting Alain. They were very close.'

'Perhaps.'

'But there's something else. She's been seeing someone else, someone she didn't tell me about.'

'How do you know?'

'We've lived together all our lives; we can account for almost every second of each other's movements.'

'How can you be sure it wasn't Jean-Pierre?'

'I saw our car going up the drive to Ste Michelle.'

'You mean – '

193

'It was amazing. I couldn't believe she would ever set foot up there. To her it was taboo. Yet I saw her driving up there.'

'Did you question her?'

'Of course.'

'And?'

'She flew into a terrible rage. Said it wasn't her – it wasn't our car.'

'And this happened once.'

'Yes. But then I saw her with someone – '

'How did you come across them?'

'I didn't. You can see the forest from the window. I often look at the old house and the forest through my binoculars. I just caught a glimpse of them through the trees.'

Marius sat silently.

'Could she have been negotiating with Alain?'

'You don't understand,' said Mireille. 'She had too much pride for that.'

'But if he were to offer – '

'Even if he did, he'd have to go on his knees to her. And why should she keep it all from me?'

'Why didn't – did you confront her over the second meeting?'

'She denied it. Again. She said I was mad and we had a terrible row.'

'And you haven't told anyone else?'

'There was no one to tell.' Mireille sounded very bleak. 'And now it's too late. But it may just be important, and you – you *know* Alain, and could – perhaps ask him?'

'Yes. I'll ring him now. While you're here.' He went to the phone and dialled Alain's number, his head swimming with confusion and fatigue.

'Yes?'

'Alain. It's Marius.'

'How are you this morning?'

'Exhausted. I've got Mireille with me.'

'I was just going down to see her.'

'She has a very strange story.'

'What's that?'

'She says Marie came to see you. Twice.'

'Good heavens!'

'Did she?'

'No.'

'The first time she saw their car disappearing up your drive; the second was when she thought she saw you walking together in the woods.'

'When was this?' His voice was crisp.

'When?' Marius lowered the receiver, turning to Mireille who looked ill at ease.

'Last week. Before – Henri was killed. I think Monday – and then Thursday.'

Marius repeated the information.

'No.' Alain was completely positive.

'She never came?'

'Don't be absurd, Marius. I'd have told you.'

'Of course you would. I'm just wondering whether she could have been visiting your couple?'

'The Descartes? Why should she? Of course I'll ask. I wish I had seen her. This – enmity – I could have done more – '

'Just a minute.' He turned to Mireille. 'Alain says he didn't see her but possibly she may have been visiting the Descartes. What do you reckon?'

'Yes, she could have been, I suppose.' She seemed suddenly thrown, flurried.

'Are you quite sure about seeing *Alain* with her in the woods?'

'I thought I was. It was only a glimpse. Maybe I was mistaken.'

'She says she may have been mistaken,' said Marius back into the receiver.

'Yes.' His voice was calm and authoritative. 'But I'll ask the Descartes. I'm surprised I didn't know about it.'

'Very strange.'

'Most odd. Will Mireille see me?'

Again Marius turned to her. 'He wants to see you.'

'Not today.' She gave a little gasp.

'Are you still staying with Annette?'

'I'm going back to her now. I'll see him – soon.'

Marius relayed the information, feeling rather weary of his role as go-between. 'She'd like to see you, soon.'

'Not today?'

'No.'

'Of course. Look, Alain – I'm going to see Didier this afternoon.'

'Would you like me to come with you?'

'That would be terrific. I'll pick you up – say about two.'

'You don't think we should check with Rodiet?'

'No,' said Marius. 'I don't. I'll see you later.' When he had put down the receiver Marius turned to Mireille. She still looked flustered.

'I've been wasting your time,' she said.

'Are you still sure it was Alain the second time?'

'No. Not now. I just thought – I'm very sorry. I feel such a fool.' Tears fell suddenly and Marius reached out to her, putting his arm around her shoulder, squeezing it awkwardly.

'It doesn't matter.'

'But it does. Involving Alain . . .'

'Maybe this will be a chance for reconciliation.'

'After what I've said?'

'Yes. He wasn't in the least put out.'

'I must go.' She stumbled to her feet.

'Are you all right? Would you like a drink?'

'No. Fatal at the moment, I'm afraid.'

'Coffee?'

'No. No, thank you. But there is one thing you *could* tell me.'

'Yes?'

'When can she be buried?'

'Soon. I gather I can make the arrangements for my father tomorrow. I don't think you'll – have to wait long.'

'Thank you.'

He showed her to the door, and watched her walk slowly away down the rutted drive. Then, deep in thought, Marius hurried back inside.

'Yes – you can see him.' This time it was another doctor but he seemed just as co-operative as the first one Marius had seen, especially when he recognised Alain as what he called 'a loyal visitor'.

'I only come twice a year – if that,' Alain protested, but the doctor, an elderly, exhausted-looking man, waved his comment away.

'You come regularly,' he said. 'That's the main thing. There are some patients who receive no visits at all.'

'Didier's had quite a lot over the last few weeks,' Marius ventured, but the old doctor ignored him.

'Can we go across ourselves?' asked Alain.

'Of course.' He looked at his watch. 'You may find him taking some exercise.'

'Where does he do that?'

'Next door to the unit. It's a few pine trees with a wall round. Still high security. It's not much but he loves it out there, especially when it's hot. He's even been out there during the siesta when the sun is really fierce.'

'How is he?' asked Alain.

'Not so good the last day or so.'

'Of course, you know him well.'

'Yes. I know Didier very well.'

Marius decided to say nothing; clearly Alain had more stature in the doctor's eyes, commanded more respect for the consistency of his visiting.

'Has anything upset him?'

'No. He just appears to be generally restless.'

'Has he said anything?'

'He told me he'd said the wrong name to someone.'

Marius felt his scalp tingle and his nerves tighten. He glanced at Alain but there was no change in his expression.

'That he'd been *told* to say the wrong name,' the doctor continued. 'And that it wasn't right. That's all I could get out of him. But he seemed most dreadfully agitated.'

Marius suddenly had a thought. 'Is Didier allowed to have telephone calls?' he said sharply.

'Yes. He is. Incoming only.'

'Does he get many?'

'I'm sorry,' said the doctor stiffly. 'I didn't realise this was an inquisition.'

'I have to say I'm a police officer.' Marius passed him his identification card.

'I see. Is this an official visit?'

'Yes.'

'Well . . .'

'It's all right,' said Alain. 'It's just that Didier knew someone in the war – someone Inspector Larche was interested in.'

'Larche – now where have I heard that name?'

'Do you log the calls?' asked Marius quickly, conscious that the doctor might bar him entry until higher officialdom had been consulted.

'We used to.'

'*Used* to?'

'Monsieur Larche, Didier has been here for over forty years – he is not considered a public enemy. No. We don't log his calls any more, and we're only too pleased when he has one.'

Alain intervened smoothly. 'I called him myself a few weeks ago – just to say hallo. I'm sorry that he's behaving oddly – '

'Yes.' The doctor was warmer again. 'It is *odd*. It's almost as if he's afraid.'

'Didier,' Alain called softly. 'Didier – it's Alain Leger.'

It was a sandy compound with a few scattered seats among the pine trees. At first Marius couldn't see him, then he picked him out – almost whited out in the sun, sitting on a bench, staring straight at the high security fence which had barbed wire strands running along its top. Did he ever remember his Maquis days, wondered Marius. Did he ever think of using his past guerilla expertise to escape? Or was Didier happy here?

'Didier,' repeated Alain softly.

Slowly he turned. A smile stretched his baby-face. 'Visitors.'

'It's Alain Leger.'

'Welcome.'

'And Monsieur Larche. He came to see you the other day.'

'Is he the shadow on the sun?'

'Sorry?'

'The shadow I see on the sun?' He spoke very slowly, as if he was savouring each word.

'I don't understand,' said Alain.

'There must never be a shadow on our Provençal sun. Not a rain cloud.' Didier giggled and then snarled. 'No shadows.'

'Didier,' began Alain.

Didier stood up and Marius felt the leaden pressure of fear. In his hand, he held a thin-bladed knife.

'Put that down,' said Alain.

'No shadows.'

'He's a friend.'

'A shadow,' repeated Didier triumphantly. 'He's going to punish Didier.'

'No,' protested Alain. 'Why should you be punished?'

'Liars must be punished. I was told to lie. And I did. And I was wrong. And when I'm wrong there's a shadow on the sun.'

'Who told you to lie?' asked Marius quietly. He had disarmed a man before, but many years ago.

'I won't say.' There was a cunning look in Didier's eyes. 'I'll have to stay here forever if I do.'

'Was it Commissaire Rodiet?'

'Who?' The cunning look was still there.

'Gabriel Rodiet.'

'I don't answer questions. Not any more. I keep quiet.' He began to circle them as Alain moved forward.

'No,' hissed Marius. 'Leave him to me.' But as he spoke Didier lunged.

Marius staggered and sweated; it was as if his entire body had become huge and immovable – as if Didier was enormously light on his feet, playing with him in a nightmarish game. He lunged and lunged again, never quite striking, his face wreathed in a beatific smile. He was chewing something. Marius could smell the bon-bon. Glancing at Alain, hovering beside him, he gasped out, 'Leave him to me. Don't get involved.'

'Marius – '

'I *said* – don't get involved.'

Didier's breathing was even as they circled and Marius' came in gasps. The sweat was so bad now in the blistering heat that it seemed to pour like a torrent into his eyes.

'Give me the knife.'

'No.'

'You'll be in here forever – '

'No. Didier won't. He won't be kept in. He's been kept in too long.'

He lunged again and this time they closed, the knife skimming Marius' wrist and drawing a little surface blood.

'Damn you.' Didier's flesh was soft and moist, spongy like a fungus. 'Alain, keep back,' Marius yelled, his fear momentarily eclipsed by revulsion at Didier's touch.

But despite his soft flabbiness, Didier seemed immensely strong and in a few seconds he was driving Marius back towards a tree, pinning him against it.

'Estelle.'

'Yes, my darling?'

'I don't feel well.' The old lady was sitting in the cool of the little sitting-room.

'Shall I get you a brandy?'

'Henri will get it.'

'He's out at the moment.'

'He's dead.'

Estelle looked up at her sharply over the newspaper she was reading in the other armchair. She had been caught out. 'Sorry.'

'I had you fooled,' said Solange triumphantly. 'Why do you lie to me?'

'I said I was sorry. Sometimes it's . . .'

'Easier?'

'Yes. But you know I care about you – '

'Yes,' said Solange vaguely. 'I sometimes feel you do.'

'Will you tell me something?'

'What?'

'Do you put some of this on?'

Solange gave her a shifty look. 'I don't know what you mean.'

'I think you do. How much do you put on?'

'Sometimes I act up a bit,' she admitted.

'I thought so. And at other times you're confused. Why do you act up, sweetheart?'

'It's easier that way.'

'Why?'

'It keeps things away – things I don't want to think about.'

'Will you tell them to Estelle?'

'I've nothing to say.'

'They'll be safe with me. All your secrets.' Estelle got up and walked over to her. She kissed Solange on the forehead. 'They'll all be safe with me,' she repeated. 'All those old secrets of yours.'

Annette and Mireille wandered alongside the rocky bed of the river. It was low, sluggish and in places almost dry. Fish moved lazily in the shallows and Mireille thought they looked bloated and obscene. How did they live in that brackish water? Why were they so fat? She kept thinking about them, trying to block out of her mind the lump of meat that had once been her sister. But the fish reminded her of that lifeless figure, and she kept seeing Marie in the water. Driftwood had piled up in the centre of the river and there was some kind of carcass on the other bank. She turned her head away abruptly. There was a smell of rotting vegetation and sour water.

'Oh God!'

Annette put her arm round her waist. 'Do you want to sit down?'

'No, let's turn inland. Away from the river.'

'It's awful in summer,' Annette agreed.

They walked down a dry, rutted path that led across a cornfield.

'Do you want to talk it all through again? Sometimes it helps just to talk it right out of one's system.' I wish I could talk André out of my system, Annette thought, wondering if she would ever feel a whole person without him.

'Yes. It'll help to talk if you can bear it. Talking keeps the horror of it out of my mind. I keep going over and over everything. If only I knew what *more* she was doing. I know it wasn't just going to see Didier, perhaps even trying to get in some ghastly blackmail partnership with Jean-Pierre. It was *more*.'

'Something to do with Ste Michelle. With revenging herself – you both – on Alain?'

'Those servants of his. I'm sure they're involved. The man – the chauffeur – perhaps that's the man I saw her with. Perhaps that's who she was going to see.'

'You must report the whole thing to Lebatre.'

201

'Yes, I'll ring him – I'll ring him when we get back. And tomorrow, of course, I must go home.'

'Soon,' said Annette. 'But not yet.'

A single rook rose over the corn and flapped slowly into the cobalt sky.

'Thank God we're away from the river,' muttered Mireille.

Kneeing him continuously in the groin, Didier drove Marius harder and harder against the pine tree, one hand on his windpipe while the other brandished the knife. Wheezing, gasping for breath, Marius told him to drop the knife, again and again, clutching at his wrist with both hands. But the smiling Didier merely pressed him harder. Out of the corner of his eye, Marius could see Alain still hovering.

'For God's sake!' he screamed out. 'Help me.'

Blunderingly, ineffectively, Alain grabbed Didier first by the shoulders and then by the waist. But he seemed to make no impression whatever.

'Go for his arm,' yelled Marius. The knife was centimetres from his throat now. 'I can't hold him off any longer.'

'I'm trying.'

'Now!' The knife was even closer – a fraction away from him. 'For God's sake. Now!'

Alain put all his weight on Didier's arm and then put a knee in the small of his back. They fell on the hard, slightly sandy soil, Alain choking, Didier giggling, whilst Marius kicked hard at his wrist and heard the sharp sound of a breaking bone. Didier stopped giggling and began to howl with pain while the knife clattered to the ground. Marius dived for it – and then hurled it far away, over the high security fence.

'You've hurt me,' sobbed Didier. 'You've hurt me.'

Didier crawled a few centimetres towards Marius, proffering his broken wrist like an animal. But Marius turned away from him. Alain was lying on the ground, grey in the face.

'Alain – '

His breathing was laboured and his lips had a bluish tinge.

'Alain!'

There was a bubble of saliva on his lips. Marius knelt down by his side, wiping the sweat from his eyes while Didier crawled round the sandy baked earth, moaning and muttering to himself.

Marius loosened Alain's collar and felt his pulse. It was like a butterfly, fluttering and darting here and there. Desperately Marius looked around him – and saw a male nurse ambling in their direction smoking a cigarette.

'You,' yelled Marius. 'Yes, you. Run!'

The man burst into a shambling trot.

Alain's throat rattled alarmingly.

'What is it?' said the nurse. He was young, callow, indecisive.

'Get a doctor – quick.'

'Why?'

'Go on – you bloody fool!' Marius roared. 'He's had a coronary – he could die.'

'We can't treat him here.'

'*What*?'

The man stuttered slightly. 'This is a psychiatric hospital. We don't have the kind of facility he needs. I'll have to get an ambulance.'

'Move,' roared Marius. 'Just bloody move.'

The ambulance swayed alarmingly as it tore round corners, its siren moaning. Alain had an oxygen mask to his face and the paramedic member was regulating a dial.

'Is he going to make it?' asked Marius. He could see that his own hands were shaking as if they had some independent life of their own.

'He's having a go.'

'Where are we going?'

'Aix.'

'God – it's miles.'

'St Esprit's closed.'

'How long?'

'Twenty minutes.'

The rocking increased and Alain opened his eyes which had been tightly shut for some time. He signalled the paramedic to take the oxygen mask off.

'Keep it on,' he said. 'You need it.'

Alain signalled more urgently.

203

'Do as he says,' snapped Marius.

'He *needs* it.'

But Alain was getting excited, trying to tug at the apparatus.

'He'll kill himself,' muttered the paramedic.

'Then take the damn thing off.'

The paramedic shrugged and started to disentangle the mask from Alain's clutching hands.

'Marius – ' His voice was indistinct, a guttural whisper.

'I'm here.'

'You know, don't you? There's no need to go to Kummel. He won't tell anyway.'

'Why not?'

'Because I've seen him – and I know he wants to go silently to his grave. He's old, ill – and believes it's all in the hands of God. He'd rather we all fought it out, like dogs with an old bone.'

'Don't talk – for God's sake don't try to talk.'

'I may die.'

'Get the mask back on.'

But Alain pushed away the thrusting hands of the paramedic. 'I *must* die. You know why, don't you?'

'Alain – '

'I'm making a full confession.'

'Not now,' Marius urged. 'Not now.'

'You must write it down.' Alain was commanding, but his breathing was becoming spasmodic.

'I can't take responsibility for all this,' stormed the paramedic. 'I don't know what the hell you're trying to – '

'Now,' said Alain. 'Get it down now.'

Marius already had his notebook out.

'I'll sign it,' whispered Alain. His breath was coming in short stabs. '*I* chaired that damnable tribunal – You knew – '

'I was beginning to wonder, Alain, but I've never wanted to solve this case. You know why, don't you? The chairman of that tribunal could equally well have been my father as far as I was concerned.'

'There was a Nazi officer murdered, the young men were executed to prevent them talking about Kummel having sex with them,' whispered Alain, ignoring Marius' intervention.

'I know all that, but I've never understood why a tribunal was necessary.'

'The Nazis – Kummel – insisted. There had to be a whitewash. Kummel would have been executed for what he did in St Esprit.'

'Why did you chair it, Alain?' asked Marius gently.

'To protect Henri. I'm sorry, Marius.' His breathing was very shallow now, but still he went on whispering – and Marius listened with growing, cold horror.

'Protect?'

'It was Henri. He procured them with Kummel. Your mother knew.'

'Father?'

'He liked boys but he went too far. He *had* to be protected. I've *always* protected him since he was a child. Maybe it was a habit.'

'You executed your *own* people?'

'They were nothing. Whores. Like Jean-Pierre. They were dragging down the honour of our country – those whores sabotaged everything our nation stood for.'

Marius began to understand. The old recluse had been living in a nationalistic past ever since the war; Ste Michelle was his sacred land, his ancient lineage and Henri was his vulnerable child, who needed the same strength of protection as the land. Alain was a walking, thinking, one-man feudal system.

His breathing worsening, Alain continued. 'After the Lyon trial – I thought it might all come out, particularly when you arrived, Marius. I didn't realise you would be so – unanxious to investigate. I thought you'd expose me and that I couldn't take.' His voice died away and Marius leaned closer. 'So when the rumours started about Henri I forced myself to help them along their way. Pure self-survival and total betrayal. I sowed the seeds with Marie first of all.'

'*Marie*? You haven't spoken to each other for years. She hated you,' said Marius in amazement.

'I had despised them – both of them – for so long. They were weak and would have despoiled Ste Michelle. But she accepted my lie – and the possibility of a share in the estate for her and Mireille,' said Alain cynically. 'But she couldn't bring herslf to tell Mireille – she's by far the stronger of the two and she might have refused to have anything to do with my dubious proposition.

'But my father – how could you kill him? After all those years of friendship and protection?'

'Henri couldn't bear the suspicion so he threatened to expose me – so much for my loyalty and friendship.'

'I don't believe you.'

'Ask your mother. She'll tell you.'

'Did she know?'

'That I killed him? She guessed – but I could never touch her. I was too fond of Solange.'

'God – '

'I was afraid that Didier might have told Jean-Pierre and Marie about me – and I was right. So I had to kill them too. He lied to you about Rodiet. He knew it was me. Always.'

'Why didn't you kill Didier?'

'How could I? He's my son. I couldn't kill him – any more than I could kill your mother.'

'Your *son*?' Marius stared at him unbelievingly.

'Yes. His mother's dead now and her identity doesn't matter.'

'Good God.'

'But Didier isn't as mad as you think. Just heavily institutionalised. I threatened him by saying I'd arranged for him to come back into the outside world if he ever told anyone. He was so terrified of leaving the hospital that he would do anything to stay inside. But I overplayed my hand and he called my bluff. He told Jean-Pierre – and begged him to stop me from persuading the authorities to release him.' Alain's breathing was coming in gasps and the paramedic shrugged his shoulders.

'Alain – ' Marius took his hand. 'Why in God's name did it matter so much? That you chaired – '

'That I did what I did? Ste Michelle – the house and its land – it's an order of life to me. Your father's homosexuality, if it came out, what I'd done – I couldn't have borne the shame. I'd rather they thought it was Henri.' He lay back and closed his eyes.

'You *really* wanted those young men to die, didn't you?' whispered Marius. 'They were scum, weren't they – in your eyes? But my father and Kummel – you let them get away with everything, didn't you? And why? Because they were men of distinction, and you respect distinction, don't you, Alain? Landowning, the ruling elite, lineage – all the so-called qualities you hold most dear – the qualities that you feel can stamp out all those impurities you don't like – all the inefficiency you saw in your sisters. Power and money and St Michelle – land and rights and ownership – that's what's important to you, isn't it? And it doesn't matter how corrupt the elite is, does it? Just as long as they keep the old French traditional life going.' Marius felt completely spent at the end of his long speech, but looking at Alain he wondered if he had been listening at all. Perhaps he was already dying.

'I'd rather die than stand trial,' muttered Alain.

'I'll bring you to trial.' There was resolution in Marius' voice at last.

'I *must* die,' said Alain. 'It's what I expected.' He smiled up at Marius – the old civilised smile. 'It would be ironic if I didn't. That trial would expose everything, wouldn't it?'

Marius nodded. 'It would damage that old order beyond repair, Alain. It might even sweep it away.'

Alain didn't die, so the irony was fulfilled. Marius was not required to see him again and was grateful. He had, however, received a short note from him. It simply read: 'I would still wish to restore Letoric. Will you allow me?'

Marius had not replied. Nor did he intend to. For he knew that Letoric must crumble away – and eventually his mother would have to be cared for elsewhere. He didn't want Alain's guilt money.

Gabriel formally charged Alain and, dependent on his recovery, a date for a trial would be set. Meanwhile he had been transferred to the hospital wing of the prison in Aix. 'He is a very frightened man,' Gabriel had told Marius. 'He is the kind of old Frenchman who treasures his privacy – his expensive privacy. Prison won't be very pleasant for him.'

Marius had not been surprised, and now, as he stood in the baking morning sun at his father's funeral, he thought of Alain – and how strong his desire for the unchanging old order had been. His gaze rose from the flower-shrouded coffin, now at rest in the open grave, to the foothills above. There, in his mind's eye, Marius saw them all – Solange, Alain, Didier, Gabriel – skulking like foxes in caves, slipping across the scree, silently moving amongst the twilit pines. They were not only fighting against the forces that had overrun their country, but were battling a far more insidious enemy. Desire. Lust. Manipulation. These were their real antagonists. His father – his own remote father – had been as great an enemy to them as the German troops whose occupation they had pledged themselves to fight. But how could they fight Henri Larche and his overriding, uncaring desires? Alain Leger had been a hero. Now he had killed more barbarically and brutally than he ever would have done in wartime conflict. And why? Because Alain had to survive. He couldn't have his Maquis image, his land, his heritage, despoiled. He had protected his closest friend – and then killed him, years later, for fear of exposure and the loss of his hard won isolation. A survivor's tactic.

The priest sprinkled holy water, the Mistral started to blow, gently at first and then harder. Marius stood with Solange and Estelle on one side, Gabriel and his wife on the other. Annette and André were there too, and standing beside Annette was Mireille. Mariola stood alone.

Marius tried to see his father in his mind but no image came to him. He was a stranger. I share his desires, thought Marius in anguish. I should be able to understand him. But, for the moment, he could no longer see him or feel his presence. Suddenly Marius could smell lavender on the wind.

THE END